Dedicated to

Aaron and Luminita, two characters who continually surprise me and forge their own backstories. With determination, they wove an incredible tale of pain and love to become two of my most complex villains. I am simply in awe of how far they've come.

Jennifer Saviano, Danny Nagel, and **Kayla Bowers**, my test bunnies, I owe you so much. Without your incredible feedback, ideas, and support I'd be lost. Thank you so much!

The Lilith Adams Series

Blood Lily
Rose of Jericho
The Lotus Tree
Ghost Orchid
Wormwood
Hellebore

Novellas from that world

Draga & the Savage: Dragobete
Draga & the Savage: Dracul – Part 1
Draga & the Savage: Dracul – Part 2
Draga & the Savage: Dracul – Part 3

For more information about permission to reproduce selections from this book, write to Permissions, Jenny Allen Books & Original Art, 872 Stoverstown Rd., York, PA, 17408

Manufacturing by Ingram Spark.
Interior Book Design by Jenny Allen
Cover Art by Blonde Design and © held by Jenny Allen.

ISBN: 979-8-9892492-4-4

Jenny Allen Books & Original Art, 872 Stoverstown Rd., York, PA 17408
JennyAllenBooks@gmail.com
www.JennyAllenBooks.com

Your mental health matters. Some may find this as a checklist of endorsements, but for those who have triggers, please read this list carefully.

Trigger Warnings:

Strong Violence & Murder
Brief depiction of the murder of minors
Attempted Sexual Assault
Drug use: Both Consensual and Non-consensual
Strong Sexual Content
Ritualistic Acts involving Blood & Sex
Depictions of War

This novella is set in Medieval Romania and uses historically accurate names, places, and Romanian words, as well as some Sumerian and Greek names.

Pronunciation/Translation Guide

Prostul moare de grija alutia (Pro-stool moor-a de gree-jah ah-loo-tee-ah)

patria protesta (pay-tree-ah pro-test-ah) male head of the family

Duklja (Doo-cool-jah) principality of Croatia

Ielele (Eye-lay-lee) Romanian lady of the woods

Moroaică (moor-ache-ah) Romanian female ghost

Zână (Zen-ah) Romanian fairy godmother

Sânziană (San-zee-ah-nah) Romanian Fairy

Dragaica (Drag-ache-ah) Romanian Lady of Flowers

Apa Sâmbetei (Ap-a Sem-bah-tee) Romanian world ocean of creation

Fîrtat (fear-taht) Romanian Brother of creation, the shining one

Nefîrtat (ne-fear-taht) Romanian Non-brother of creation

Dumuzid (Doom-ah-zid) Sumerian god of agriculture/shepards

Enmesarra (En-mes-sar-rah) Sumerian God of the Underworld

Ninazu (nin-ah-zoo) Sumerian God of healing

Penchenegs (Pen-cha-negs) semi-nomadic Turkish people

Strigoi (stree-goy) a Romanian vampire

Sălbatic (sal-bah-tic) Romanian for "savage"

Tocană (toe-cah-no) a hearty Romanian stew

Timisoara (Tee-mee-sow-ah-rah) Romanian city along the Timis river

Mureş (Mur-esh) Romanian river

Dunăre (Doo-nah-ray) Romanian river

Dacians (Da-key-ans) An ancient Agrarian society in Dacia (Romania)

Dragobete (Drag-oh-beat) Romanian festival of love and fertility

Meu (mew) Romanian for "my"

Ahhazu (Ah-ha-zoo) Female Akkadian demon who spread disease

Erinyes (Err-in-yeah-s) Greek demigods of vengeance

cioareci (too-yar-rich) A type of woolen pants worn in medieval times

Mărțișor (Mah-see-shore) Spring festival of fertility and rebirth

Măselarița (Meh-sah-la-ree-sha) Romanian for Henbane plant

Mătrăguna (Mah-trah-goo-nah) Romanian for Atropa Belladonna plant

Decidava (Deck-e-dah-vah) Ancient Romanian city

Draga &
The Savage:
Dragobete

by Jenny Allen

J.A.
Books

Jenny Allen Books
York, PA 17408

.

1. The Fool

Luminita

The Romanians have a saying. *Prostul moare de grija alutia*—The fool dies worrying about someone else. Most see that as a proverb to not stick one's nose where it doesn't belong. I, however, see another meaning. Concern for others will lead to your destruction. I've watched the lesson play out many times over my long life, but none so poignant as the downfall of my father, Dragomir of Duklja.

I was born near the Bay of Kotor shortly before it fell under Bulgarian rule. It was a pretty enough place, nestled in the hills overlooking the Adriatic Sea, but like most of Europe in the Middle Ages, it was violent.

My cousin Jovan Vladimir ruled the Durand families in Serbia and Croatia. He also governed the Duklja principality in general until the Bulgarian's invaded. Samuel, the intruders' Emperor, imprisoned my cousin for a time, but Jovan was a resourceful man with a particular gift. He had a…way with the ladies and won the heart of the emperor's daughter.

With the assistance of his love, Theordora, they persuaded Samuel to release Jovan and the emperor allowed him to serve as his vassal in Duklja. Things were less turbulent for a time, but never peaceful. In 1016, my cousin was beheaded by Ivan Vladislav—the Bulgarian successor to Samuel's son—in front of a church in Prespa. The act sparked my disdain for the *houses of God*, despite the church recognizing Jovan as a martyr and a saint. What good does honor serve a dead man? It only assuages the guilt of the living, and poorly at that.

After the death of our *patria protesta*…the head of our Durand family, my father Dragomir was placed in charge, but we were forced to flee our home, chased out by the new Bulgarian emperor. We lived a simple life with my father's soldiers during our brief exile, but it was a happier one.

Although being a noble made life as a Durand easier, allowing us to feed on the emotions of those under our control, it also made us targets…the men at least. My father and my brother Stefan were always in the limelight. As a young woman, I was only valued as a bargaining chip, if I was valued at all. The lack of my name appearing in the histories is testament to that.

The inability to control my fate didn't take long to become a festering wound. While Stefan had all the advantages, I was frequently forgotten or seen as a burden…another mouth to feed. It didn't matter that I had a keener strategic mind than my brother. *Women have no place in power*, my father often reminded me.

The fool should have taken my council. I would have warned him that the Kotorans he was so worried about, bore him no good will. My father insisted that he had a duty to the humans who had served his nephew Jovan. *Prostul moare de grija alutia.*

In 1018, Dragomir left us along with his soldiers in an idiotic mission to establish himself as rightful ruler of Duklja and free his people. His campaign saw some success until he came to our home of Kotor. The town welcomed him with open arms and prepared a banquet in Dragomir's honor. The peasants were smart, placating his inflated ego and sense of righteousness, but they had not forgotten our sins. They were not aware of our nature…our ability to sense and consume emotion, but they still saw us as greedy, lecherous nobles.

My father attended the banquet with only a handful of his men, believing the lies the Kotorans spewed, soaking in their praise like a starving animal. I have no doubt he truly thought he had saved them. While we'd lived there, he'd never noticed the sly glances and hateful glares. That is the one advantage to being invisible, ignored by society, treated as nothing but a pretty possession. I'd witnessed all their true faces, their unguarded hatred and jealousy.

Sadly, Dragomir did not that night, even with his Durand abilities. They attacked him and his men. After he escaped the banquet, my father took refuge in a church, *of all things*. As if the Christian God spreading across the empire would somehow take pity and save him. If such a thing ever existed, it did not answer my father's prayers. The Kotorans stoned him to death right there…in the bowels of a church. There were no honors bestowed on his corpse.

When the news reached our family, I decided to head out on my own. I would not allow the sentimentality and greed of my brother to bring about *my* death. I would not hand over my fate to lesser men any longer. I would rather live in the woods than suffer their idiotic campaigns.

Stefan went on to succeed where my father had failed, fighting not only the Bulgarians, but revolting against the Byzantine empire. However, I did not stay to witness his deeds. I traveled northeast toward the Carpathian Mountains into the Kingdom of Hungary and the region of Transylvania. Legends followed in my wake. A beautiful woman luring men into the woods with enchanting dances…a woman with flowers who either granted wishes or destroyed men, depending on her mood…a fairy with enchanting abilities…

They gave me many names…Ielele, moroaică, Zână, Sânziană…but Dragaica, The Lady of Flowers, was the one that stuck.

2. The Weak

Aaron

The creation myth from Romania is one of my favorites, perhaps because it speaks to me, mirroring my history as the first born and my diametric relationship with my brother Gregor.

The legend states that in the beginning, before time and matter, only a boundless ocean existed...*Apa Sâmbetei*. For eons, the surface remained as placid as glass...a mirror reflecting the heavens. A ripple appeared first. The ocean began to churn violently, creating waves that whipped the sea into a frothy foam. From the depths, a massive tree emerged, its majestic limbs unfurling.

Along its branches crawled two creatures—a butterfly and a worm. The butterfly shed its wings of ethereal beauty and transformed into a beautiful boy, the shining one, *Fîrtat*. The worm, in its jealously, wriggled and writhed, shedding its body to become a boy as well, but something less...something clouded in darkness, *Nefîrtat*.

"Brother!" the second boy exclaimed while moving to embrace the first, but the shining one grimly shook his head.

"You are not my brother, for I can have no equal. I shall call you, Nonbrother."

Jenny Allen

I always found it amusing that Gregor—Dumuzid as he was originally named—identified with the first brother. He felt his loyalty and devotion to good embodied the spirit of Brother, the shining one. He failed to see the point of the story.

I was born first. I held no illusions about my power and the role humans played in my life. I never tried to be something I was not. At least, not until my hand was forced centuries later. The shining light is not about good versus evil. It is about truth versus self-deception. See, *Nefirtat* was a mimic. He was shrouded in darkness because he couldn't see his own truth.

Dumuzid was always Nonbrother. He played the part of a Sumerian god, a human, a shepherd…but never embraced his true nature. We are vampires, not anything else, and I alone reveled in that role. I always thought that was why the sun never burned me the way it did to Gregor and Duncan. I alone lived in the daylight, like the shining one. I embodied *Firtat*.

Even the Sumerians associated me with truth and death. As Enmesarra, they portrayed me as their god of the Underworld, a judge of the dead. It was quite fitting. Before the concept of judge, jury, and executioner existed, I fulfilled those roles.

Duncan preferred to stay out of the conflicts between me and my brother. He spent his time tinkering, creating, studying…ignoring everything else. The Sumerian people did go to him seeking cures, however. He typically indulged them, but *only* because of the scientific challenge. They named him Ninazu, the Lord of healing. The man saw his heritage as a *condition* to be maintained. He was practical that way. We disagreed on the matter, but at least he never pretended to be anything other than himself.

The myth *after* the initial creation of Brother and Nonbrother had a more direct and undeniable correlation to Gregor and I. See, *Firtat*, the shining one, molded an island for the cosmic tree since he could not swim. This exerted him, and he laid under its branches to rest. *Nefirtat* saw an opportunity to create his own world, free from the shadow of his elder brother. He tried to roll him into the sea…to drown him.

Draga & the Savage: Dragobete

After the fall of Sumerian civilization, we traveled slowly Northeast and eventually made a home in the Carpathian Mountains centuries later. It took thousands of years for Gregor to finally work up his nerve. He'd had enough of my voracious appetite. The myths of the Strigoi unnerved him. He argued that humans would eventually rise against us and cause our destruction if I continued to indulge my dark urges.

I ignored his pathetic pleas to blend in. We were not human. We existed to mold the world the way we saw fit. Gregor, or Gavril as he was known at that time, had other plans, and I was in the way. During the chaos of the Hungarian conflict with the Holy Roman Empire, Gregor attempted to free himself from my shadow. Instead of rolling me into the sea, he waited until I went out hunting, and sent a band of Hungarian soldiers to end my life. They died screaming my brother's name.

I should have ended Nonbrother after that. I still don't understand why I didn't. Perhaps because we were alone in the world, or so we thought. We had no knowledge of other vampires at that time. We were gods among the weak, whether or not Gregor chose to believe that. We were meant to flourish, to expand our reach. So, when Gregor and Duncan stole away in the night sometime during the 11th century, I let them.

I had no strings to hold me back after that. I indulged myself amid the continual conflicts and snuck into huts under the cover of night. The Hungarians, the Romans, the Penchenegs, local villagers...I didn't care about sides. Their blood all tasted the same.

The legend of Strigoi ran rampant and people employed all manner of odd charms to keep me at bay. Thorns placed on the thresholds and windowsills were a particular favorite of mine. As if tiny barbs would stop *me*. Their garlic and onion braids, offerings of pig's blood, and religious icons were amusing, yet ineffective, of course.

In 1241, the Mongol's Golden Horde descended on us with vicious devastation. They destroyed entire villages, slaughtered thousands, and I was...inspired. The time for creeping through the dark had come to an end. I stayed near their path, hiding my bloody delights among their atrocities, and the fulfillment of my vampiric destiny…culling the weak…made my soul sing.

However, even within the blood-drunk haze of indulgence, I didn't realize my true potential until a chance encounter revealed it to me… until I earned the name *Sălbatic*—the Savage.

3. The Timis

Early Spring 1241
Luminita

Tonight, there is a chill in the spring air, but the meager fire in my clay stove and the hot stew warm my bones as I gaze across the river Timis to the fortified town overlooking it. The light from torches and fires twinkle in the dark like stars.

I am primarily nocturnal for two reasons. First, I am less likely to encounter humans. Most of them are securely tucked away in their stove-warmed huts after sundown. As a woman living alone, encounters can be...precarious.

Second, if someone does happen upon me, they are more likely to mistake me for an ethereal being...something not of this world. Perhaps mistake is not the correct word. Identify would be more appropriate. I do exist above the natural laws of humans, after all.

I've watched many of them whither into shriveled husks while tilling fields, hunting prey, and struggling for every meager scrap of food. They are a pitiful race designed to procreate and consume until their short lives run out. It's difficult to understand a point to their existence, except perhaps, as part of the greater food chain.

However, there are power in numbers, so I limit my interactions to bartering in town for goods only when needed. The ability to read emotions is a rather handy trick that amuses the common people as long as it remains innocuous. Anything too foreboding would likely end with me on a stake, and I am not fireproof. I avoid pointing out the adulterers, thieves, and violent ones. I stick to telling the pretty ladies that a particular boy might seek their affection or predicting a pregnancy they aren't yet aware of…harmless things of that nature.

The emotional energy I require is easily enough obtained, either from these readings or entertaining wanderers lost in the woods and travelers along the dark roads. I've discovered that the more I draw from these humans, the less need I have of physical nourishment, but I have always been fond of a hearty *tocană*. The rich stew brimming with meat and vegetables warms the blood on nights like tonight.

About ten years ago, I settled into this abandoned hut tucked into the woods. It had once been used as temporary lodging for long hunts, especially during the vicious winters. But shortly after my arrival, rumors spread of restless spirits and unfriendly fairy folk. It was quickly abandoned, and most are frightened to venture too close.

A twig snaps in the dark, echoing through the vacant woods and pulling me from my thoughts. *Most are frightened, but not all.* After eating another spoonful of vegetables and mutton, I slide my bowl close to the stove, so it stays warm. Apparently, a performance is in order.

I lay my blanket across the rough-hewn chair and smooth out my sheer crimson dress, one of the few things I've kept from my former life. I never wear it in town, of course, but I frequently don it at night. When people stumble across me in the wild, the lavish and provocative garment fortifies their belief in my powers. It identifies me as something… more.

Another distant sound draws my attention to the woods. They are quite far out, coming from the South. It's unlikely they're from town. Probably a traveler of some sort…someone who might not be missed. A grin tugs at my lips as I slip silently into the woods.

Night blooming jasmine scents the air, making it sweet, and a full moon paints the forest in pale light and deep shadows. A perfect night for a hunt. I glide down paths familiar only to me, past the vast sea of beech trees. At the large oak, I adjust my course, and slow my approach. The sounds of multiple travelers reach my ears…feet marching through the brush, and I pause. Power in numbers.

After shrouding myself in the deep shadows of an elm, I close my eyes and concentrate, reaching out with my Durand senses. The signatures appear in my mind one by one until over two dozen are revealed. This is far more than a few travelers lost in the woods and they are all fixated on one thing—violence.

I quickly head west. Two dozen men or more is not a fair fight, and I don't want to lead them back to my humble abode. The night air seems colder now. I should have brought the blanket, or perhaps it has nothing to do with the weather.

As I pick my way through the trees and bramble, I notice four signatures diverting from the pack…heading in my direction. I was certain my steps were too quiet to be noticed, but if they are following me, I suppose not. If only I'd used my senses sooner, identified the threat before I was too close to escape unscathed. But there is still time. They haven't caught me yet, and four presents far less of a challenge. Under the right circumstances, it's barely a challenge at all.

I weave between pockets of shadow, frequently altering my course, and the four men continue to follow at an easy pace. The night drags on this way…a delicate dance between us. By the time they start to advance, quickening their pace, I reach the edge of a clearing. This is my opportunity to get a proper look at them.

After a moment of indecision, I sprint across the open space. The moonlight makes me clearly visible, but my speed is something I doubt they can match. Once I reach the other side, I sink into the shadows and wait.

The night grows still, as if the forest itself is holding its breath. The only sounds are the marching feet growing rapidly closer. Then branches begin to move along the clearing's edge, and four men step into the moonlight. They pause, dark eyes fixed on my location. Each of them is clad in heavy armor composed of iron scales and thick leather. The cone shaped helmets and long wispy facial hair identify them as part of the

Mongol horde rumored to be invading from the south, and now they're here…*in my home.*

Facing four peasants is a situation I would typically avoid, but four battle-hardened soldiers with vicious-looking swords strapped to their belts… I could try to outrun them. The armor and weaponry should slow them down, but I have nowhere safe to run. If the horde was marching North, Timisoara, the fortress on the hill, will surely fall.

The men begin to advance, eyes searching the dark as they creep through the clearing. We are far enough west that if I lead them back toward the Timis, we would be some distance away from their army. Perhaps the river would aid my escape. The water is frigid this time of year, but I can swim it. These men in their heavy gear cannot.

The decision made, I bolt, crashing through the woods as fast as my feet will carry me. The men lose all pretense and tear after me. They're much faster than I thought they'd be.

For the first time in decades, true fear pumps through my veins. My heart thrashes against my ribs and each breath burns in my lungs as I push to run faster. I know I cannot keep this pace for long and the river is still too far.

Violent humans and their idiotic wars. How many leaders of these victories live to see the lands they conquer and for how long? A year? Perhaps five if they aren't assassinated? I've already lived sixty times that, and I'll survive much longer. These soldiers will not be *my* undoing.

Fatigue sets in and my pace slows. The men are gaining. I can hear the river, but they'll catch me before I reach it.

I can see the moonlight ahead…the forest's edge…and it spurns me on. Every scrap of energy goes into reaching that line, but the sounds behind me are growing louder. They're closing in and I sense all the horrible intentions emanating from them as if they are flaming arrows in the dark.

Just as I break through into the moonlight, a heavy body slams into me, sending me flying forward. I don't hesitate. I twist and squirm while the man paws at me, groping and grabbing. Every touch makes bile rise in my throat. *No human* deserves to touch me in such a way.

Draga & the Savage: Dragobete

With determination burning in my gut, I kick and fight my way out from under the man, clawing at the earth until I'm free. It only lasts an instant. Hands grab my arms and hair, pulling me to my feet, and I spare one momentary glance at the river's tumultuous surface.

The men yell in guttural tones, but I don't understand their words. Still, I feel every lecherous impulse slide over my skin. The panic gripping my chest eases at that, and a slow smile spreads my lips. These men think I'm an easy target, but I can inspire as much terror as their intimidating visage if not more. Humans are easily frightened by things they can't explain.

After twisting my wrist, I latch on to the soldier to my right, digging my nails into the leather, and pull. I draw on every single wisp of energy his body contains, viciously ripping it away at the root. The man stumbles, releases me, and then falls.

Incredulous shouts accompany their sudden shock and fear, and power thrums seductively beneath my pale skin. My eyes drift up to the full moon with renewed purpose and I chant it's praises in my native tongue.

Cold steel meets my throat and I fall quiet, but it doesn't summon the terror they desire. My nails bite into the man's hand and I turn to stare at him, the blade breaking my skin in the process. His beady eyes widen at the blood trickling down my neck before he meets my murderous glare. I dig my nails deeper, drawing blood, and I tear away every emotion, consuming each of them until nothing remains. The knife falls to the ground with a thud and then the man's lifeless body follows.

The soldier gripping my hair releases me with a stream of indecipherable words and backs up to his only remaining companion. I could let them run. They are properly terrified and have no desire to get any closer. But I am not in a forgiving mood, and I do not wish them to bring reinforcements back to hunt me.

I take a step closer and both men draw their swords. Fear infuses the night air. The scent is more intoxicating than the night blooming jasmine and I breathe it deep into my lungs. The full moon draws my attention once more and the chant spills from my lips like silk. Then my piercing gaze falls to the trembling men before me.

"You have angered Dragaica," I say, though I know they do not understand.

A quick darting motion to the left makes them jump back with an amusing scream and my grin widens. Another dart to the left has the same effect, positioning them right where I want them. As I saunter closer, my fingers capture the rivulet of blood tracing my neck. I watch them take several awkward steps backward while I slowly lick the sticky blood from my fingers.

Their mouths open in shrieks of horror. Simpletons.

Without warning, I sprint for them, and their boots hit the crumbling bank of the river Timis. Recognition hits, and their swords fall to the ground as they try to throw themselves forward. Both do not succeed.

While one splashes into the turbulent water with a scream, the other claws at the bank, digging his fingers into the earth. I slowly make my way toward him, pausing only to pick up his sword. The moonlight shimmers across the metal hypnotically.

The man utters a string of hasty words. Even if I understood them, they'd mean nothing. This one…touched me in places no one should without my permission. After a few more steps, I crouch down, bringing my face close to his.

Pleading panic burns his eyes with tears. He wants mercy when he would have shown me none. How amusing. His eyes follow me as I slowly stand to my full height. More begging gibberish escapes his mouth, but it only brings a delirious grin to my face.

In a swift motion, I draw the sword over my head and his eyes widen. With all my strength I bring the blade down, severing his hand at the wrist. Blood sprays across the dirt in rhythmic spurts and screams fill my ears like beautiful music. I draw the sword over my head again, hot splashes of blood flinging from the blade.

The soldier yells incomprehensible words, but I slash down at his remaining hand. The shrill shrieks are interrupted by the splash, replaced by gurgled cries as the current takes him away. I watch until his iron helmet disappears beneath the surface.

4. The Horde

Aaron

The brilliant light of the full moon peeks between the leaves and cuts through the dark in sharp beams while I stalk the marching horde. Despite using the cover of night, the Mongols stomp through the forest like wild beasts, creating more than enough noise for me to track them and still maintain a safe distance.

A plume of fog accompanies each of my heavy breaths. It's colder than usual for this time of year, but excitement still heats my blood, fending off the chilly bite in the spring air. After the army decimated the last village, I'd snuck in and eliminated any survivors. Drinking my fill and sating my sadistic urges without fear of repercussion was... exhilarating.

The way their tender flesh gave way beneath my teeth and fangs, the pervasive scent of coppery blood flooding the air, the firelight flickering in their eyes as they dimmed, the tears streaking through the mud and crimson covering their cheeks... Humans are so deliciously fragile.

Once I'd indulged myself, it didn't take long to catch up to the marching horde. They left an obvious trail of devastation in their wake, slaughtering anyone in their path. While I admire their ruthlessness, the hunter in me wishes tracking them presented more of a challenge.

The rushing sound of a river reaches my ears and I pause to calculate our position. We're too far south for it to be the Mureş and we crossed the Dunăre before the last attack. This has to be the Timis, or the Temes as outsiders often call it.

Over the past hundred years since Gregor and Duncan left, I've explored every inch of Romania, never staying too long in one place. The population is ever changing. The Mongols are not the first to invade and the influx of settlers from the Hungarian, Germanic, Saxon, and Polish territories have brought a wealth of diverse beliefs. However, the legend of the strigoi has remained ever-present, an evil spirit drinking the blood of wayward souls. That is until the past year…my one regret with my current situation.

Utilizing the army's devastation to hide my more savage urges affords me freedom from persecution, but also denies me recognition. I take a certain pride in cultivating the horrifying myths which surround me. After all, I should be feared after seven thousand years of blood and death. That is my legacy, although it's been attributed to many names over the years—Wepwawet, Arawn, Empusa, Lamia, Striges, Shtriga, Vetalas, Alukah, and others I can no longer recall.

Sometime ago, I adopted the Herbrew name Aaron, perhaps due to my fond memories of Ancient Wales as Arawn, a god of the hunt and the underworld. Still, no one calls me by the name. I don't see the point in forming attachments. Humans live so briefly, and I no longer speak with my brothers. Who would I tell my name? It would be forgotten within a generation, like so many before this one.

The roar of the river grows louder and the Mongol army drifts east, most likely heading for a bridge or a safe place to cross. I sneak up to the forest's edge and peer between the leaves. On a hill overlooking the Timis sits a town with fortified walls—Timisoara. I've visited this place many times over the years, though I can't recall my last appearance. Fifty years maybe…sixty.

The Mongols march across a narrower stretch of river farther down, but the area is exposed. There are no trees to hide me. Staying in the forest would be the safest bet. I can watch them sack the town from here,

Draga & the Savage: Dragobete

wait until they move on, and then my fun can truly begin. The fangs folded to the roof of my mouth ache in anticipation.

As I venture a little farther from my spot, a muted flicker of light captures my attention. It seems too close to be a torch or lantern from the Mongols. Is someone else lurking out here in the dark? A wicked grin curls my lips at the thought. Perhaps I don't have to wait after all. Maybe I can entertain myself while the Horde plunders the town.

With slow, silent footsteps, I creep toward the light until a modest hut comes into view. Faint firelight flickers from the windows, but as I watch, no shadows move within the structure. It's possible the inhabitants are asleep. It is rather late.

I don't bother being quiet when I approach the hovel. No one inside could pose a threat to me and if they happen to wake…it only heightens the fun. Still, there are no signs of movement inside, which is disappointing. Perhaps the Mongols already eradicated the home's inhabitants.

Irritation itches beneath my skin as I swing the door open to an empty hut. A fire burns low in a clay stove with a pot on top and a bowl of stew sitting beside it to stay warm. A blanket lays over a roughhewn chair facing the window looking out over the river and the town beyond. A modest bed of straw lies undisturbed in the corner, rich fabrics tumble from a wooden box nearby, and a wide variety of herbs hang from the ceiling.

The Mongols most certainly did not find this place, so where is its owner? Its rather *eclectic* owner is a woman, judging by the rare garments peeking from the trunk. Most of them are items I've only seen along the coast of the Adriatic, and some are rather old.

The stew lures me inside with its hearty scent. I haven't had real food since yesterday and now I'm acutely aware of my empty stomach. The occupant has an excellent view of the town. I can eat, stay warm, and observe the carnage from a safe distance. Perhaps the woman who lives here will return before the army moves on. One can hope. I'm hungry for more than stew.

5. Intruder

Luminita

After the attack, I huddled in the shadows of the tree line, clutching the bloody sword until my fingers grew numb. Now, from my vantage point, I can see the flames engulfing parts of the town, sending billowy clouds of black smoke into the breaking dawn. I don't dare venture closer, not until I know the horde has moved on. Taking down four soldiers had been enough excitement for one evening, and my hut sits far too close to the town for my comfort.

The energy I stole from them still riots through my body like snakes in a barrel, urging me to take action, but my mind is far stronger. I was lucky last night. Any more than four soldiers and one might have gotten away. If the army catches wind of a creature in the woods who can eat souls, they'll burn the forest to ash to find me.

I watch in relief as the Mongols begin to march out of the city, heading north...away. When I try to stand, my legs fail me at first. The muscles scream in protest, but I dig the sword into the ground and use it to drag myself upright. After several minutes, my body adjusts and I'm able to take a few unsteady steps. I should have changed positions during the night. If someone had happened upon me... *Always prepared, always vigilant, always in control.* That is my mantra, my way of life.

Jenny Allen

Slowly and quietly, I pick my way through the woods, staying close to the river, keeping an eye on the city. Small bands frequently veer off to explore, especially if the main army decides to make camp close by. The path up to Timisoara remains vacant for most of my trek. When I get close to my home, however, I see a lone figure on the hill, strolling toward the burning city, and it captures my attention. Why would anyone calmly walk *toward* a ransacked city unless they are completely oblivious or blind and deaf? I can hear the screams from here.

I turn my attention away from the strange figure and continue on, but when I arrive at the small clearing surrounding my hut, I freeze. The door is open, and I distinctly remember closing it last night.

After slipping behind a beech tree, I close my eyes and stretch my senses. There is no one inside, but there was... I can sense the imprint, the emotions so intense, they leave a mark. It's a rather unique ability. All Durand can sense emotions from someone within their range, but none that I know of can feel what they've left behind...except me.

What I sense piques my interest. The violent urges are easily enough explained, but they originated from *one* person. Soldiers are unlikely to wander off alone, as I was reminded last night. Then there is the old hunger...the ancient hunger that is not so easily explained, and... curiosity, excitement.

When I stroll inside, I notice the bowl and pot of stew are empty, the blanket lies on the floor beside the chair which is closer to the window now, and someone has rifled through my clothing. Whoever was here, a man I think, stayed for quite some time.

I wander to the window, gazing up at Timisoara, but the strange figure is no longer visible. Screams continue to fill the air despite no more movement from the Mongol horde. How very curious.

Instinct dictates that I either hide in my home or travel south, away from the invaders, but the dying town on the hill calls to me. The signature left behind in my home is...unique, something I've never come across and I'm intrigued. I wonder if it's the same curiosity the stranger felt in my home. Could he somehow sense I am different? I would suspect another Durand, but that hunger...the primal craving for violence...it is not something I've sensed in one of my kind.

Draga & the Savage: Dragobete

Suddenly, the exertion of last night hits me like a wave and the sword clangs to the packed dirt floor. For all my strengths and abilities, sleep is still a necessity, unfortunately. After retrieving the sword from the ground once more, I use it to reinforce the closed door. It won't protect me from an intruder but should wake me and provide time to prepare.

Before I can collapse on my cot, however, there is something else I must do. I fight off the drowsiness long enough to cut down a bundle of dried sage. The smoldering coals in my clay stove have just enough heat to light the herbs. I blow on the smoldering end, watching the embers glow bright, and a heady smoke fills the small space.

The Dacians have used this ritual for some time to cleanse and purify. It does seem to help fade the imprints left behind and calm me. I may not believe in certain magics, but rituals have power…intention has power. I've seen evidence of that many times in my life.

Once I've filled every corner with the savory smoke and opened the windows for a time, I toss the bundle's remnants into the stove and lie down on my bed. The small hut feels peaceful, quiet, even tranquil as it lulls me into a well-deserved sleep.

When I awake a few hours later, my mind is set. Vivid dreams left me with a burning desire to know who invaded my space. The sun hangs low with vibrant hues of pink and orange marred by the billowing black smoke from the ransacked town. The fires have gone out and I no longer hear screams.

I change into slightly more suitable traveling attire—a simple white shift and a black vest embroidered with colorful flowers. I use my blanket to bundle a selection of clothes, including my sheer crimson dress, and toss in several bundles of sage and various herbs for the upcoming spring celebration of Dragobete.

The "day when the birds are betrothed" is one of my favorites, and no matter where I am, I've indulged the traditions for some time. Boys and girls of age flood the forest on those days in search of snowdrop and crocus flowers. The carefree celebration of Spring is a rare moment in their short and brutal lives. Although, I still struggle to understand the odd tradition of stepping over a partner's foot to establish dominance in the relationship. I've often wondered where that one originated…how it came to be…its significance.

After shaking off the random thought, I pack the modest bits of bread and cheese the stranger left untouched. One more scan of the hut, reminds me to grab the gold belt, bands, and necklace I keep hidden beneath my straw bed. Then I use a silk cord to bind the pack and create straps for me to carry it easier.

Ten years this place has been my home, my sanctuary, but the temptation to experience something new…something I've never come across is far too enticing. Perhaps it is nothing, and I will return to this place. Or perhaps it is everything, and I will never look back.

The path leading up to the smoldering town is wrought with signs of war. The bodies become less sporadic the closer I get to the once fortified walls. The scent of burning flesh and blood taints the evening air. None of this is new to me. The world is a violent place, and humans are capable of more atrocities than the evil spirits they fear. What does capture my attention, however, is the silence. It's unnatural and eerie in a place typically filled with an abundance of noise.

The Mongols are not known for leaving survivors. This is true, but my desire for knowledge has me hoping a clever little human hides somewhere in the wreckage. The lone figure I saw cresting the hill toward the city may not even be the one who took refuge in my hut, but some bit of his essence clings to this path. It's faint, almost instinctual rather than an actual sense, but it draws me into the violent remains of Timisoara.

The carnage contained within the walls rivals the bloodiest of my memories. Hacked bodies litter the ground. At first, its only males… soldiers, but the farther I venture in, the more that changes. Women and children are huddled together in bloody piles and their charred corpses lie near smoldering huts and hovels. Everything was set ablaze. There is not a single structure left untouched.

Holding my sleeve to my nose to mute the wretched stench, I pick my way through the town. The hem of my shift is already crimson from the blood-soaked ground.

Draga & the Savage: Dragobete

When I round the empty stables, something odd catches my notice. A woman lies dead on the strewn hay, but her injuries are not consistent with the carnage thus far. There are no sword wounds, arrows, or burns. There is only a bloody mark on her neck and chest. After inching closer, I take some of the water from the trough and splash it across the wounds.

Matching crescent-shaped marks mar her neck and chest with two small but deep punctures. Immediately, my mind leaps to the legend of the strigoi, a creature that drinks the blood of humans typically with a bite in these particular places. I never put much stock in the myth, but now a thrill of excitement courses through my veins. If the stories are true…it might explain the ancient hunger I sensed in my hut.

A subtle shuffling sound breaks the grave-like silence, and my head whips toward the stable. It could be an animal, though most seem to have been slaughtered or taken. I don't move. Instead, I reach out with my senses and am greeted by a rather pleasant surprise. Overwhelming fear and sadness emanate from deep inside the half-burned structure.

Slowly, I rise and step closer with my palms held out. "I do not wish to harm you," I say in the local dialect.

The shuffling sounds seem a bit closer this time and I continue forward. "I only wish to help find the people who did this."

"Not people," a soft little voice replies from inside.

"Oh? What did this?"

Dark eyes half hidden by a curtain of black curls peeks from the doorway. The girl seems to be no more than seven. "Dragaica?" Her mouth falls open in surprise and her eyes become impossibly wide.

I crouch down with a reassuring smile. "Yes, little one. What happened here?"

The girl's gaze falls to the bloody straw. "First, the soldiers came. I hid in the stable with my mother and sisters, but then…" Tears gather along her thick lashes and roll down her tanned cheeks. "…the monster came."

"The monster?" I ask curiously.

The girl nods her head before her eyes dart around, as if expecting someone to attack at any moment.

"What did this monster look like?"

Her gaze snaps back to me. "It pretended to be a man. Long dark hair, silver eyes, but he had two long teeth…longer than the rest. He bit them…stole their blood." The girl cowers against the door frame, her eyes wildly scanning the area again.

"It is okay, child. The monster has fled. He is no longer here." I hold my arms out, inviting her closer.

Timidly, she steps out of the stable and ventures closer.

"That's it, little one. I will save you from the monster."

More tears roll down her cheeks as she runs into my open arms with a little sob.

"Shh…everything will be okay now. Peace will find you." Straw falls from her hair while my hands gently stroke the soft curls.

Her little arms wrap around my neck, squeezing as she cries.

I close my eyes, drawing in her grief and misery, stealing it from her bit by bit. The crying begins to stop but I keep pulling at her essence, drinking it in. She goes quiet, then still, then her arms slip from my neck as I take the last dredges of her spirit.

After I lower her to the straw, I close her lifeless eyes. Some may consider the act cruel, but she would face far worse on her own and I require energy if I am to track the strigoi while avoiding the Mongols. Better I utilize her life for a greater purpose than allow her to wander into the wilderness to die of starvation. *That* would be a painful tragedy and a waste of her short life.

6. Consequences

Aaron
Orăștie

I don't have to kill in order to get what I need. In fact, one human contains more blood than I can drink in a single attack. The practical reason I end their lives is to eliminate retribution. A dead person can't gather a group and storm the castle, so to speak. The impractical reason is…I enjoy it.

I watch the life leave the woman's eyes. This one's blood tasted almost earthy beneath the coppery tang. Quite delicious. A feeling of satisfaction washes over me. It's short-lived, like always, but nothing else quenches the darkness in me. It's like a writhing snake inside my head, which only stills when it's fed properly. In that one shining moment, the world is at peace…I am at peace, as if fulfilling some small sliver of my greater purpose.

A shriek fills the decimated town center of Orăștie, and I unceremoniously drop the body, whirling toward the sound. I only catch a glimpse of the child as it disappears around the smoldering corpse of a church. I should have completed my search of the town before indulging myself.

Hopefully, the child is the only one still alive. The Mongols haven't left many stragglers behind in the previous towns. They'd only left me one in Timisoara, much to my disappointment.

Silently, I slip around the opposite side of the church, hoping to cut off the tiny human's escape. Smoke still rises from the walls, and they radiate a sweltering heat. Sweat beads across my skin, soaking my bloody linen shirt and trailing down my back. Footsteps pound closer, and I pick up my pace to intercept.

A mop of dark hair appears, and I lunge, seizing the child around the waist and hauling them up. Shrill screams echo through my skull as the thing flails in my arms. The small ones are always so loud. It kicks and bites like a rabid beast. A surge of impatience tears through me and I snap the thing's neck. The town falls blissfully silent once again.

Gregor asked me once if I felt any remorse when killing a child. I found the question rather odd. After the first thousand years, all humans seemed like children. Their life spans are so brief. Does it truly matter if I snuff them out at age six or sixty? It's all a blink of an eye to me.

Gregor, of course, thought my answer monstrous. He truly believes in preserving the innocence of children. I still struggle to understand why. They only grow up to be greedy, loathsome things. Life robs them of their innocence regardless. Where is the sense in "preserving" it, delaying the inevitable? My brother spends far too much time living and loving among humans.

Pounding footsteps interrupt my thoughts…*several* sets. Apparently, the horde didn't linger here the way they had at Timisoara. After slaughtering those in the open, they must have lit the fires and moved on. I can differentiate at least nine sets, all running toward the once-screaming child now limp in my arms. A weary sigh rushes past my lips. I drop the broken thing before I sprint around the church, heading for the path out of town. There are power in numbers, and I am not immune to damage.

When my boots hit the packed dirt road, a chorus of shouts and screams emanate from behind me. They're far closer than I'd hoped, but I don't waste precious time glancing behind me. A rock sails by head to land in the dead grass. I push harder, running for the tree line just beyond the wrecked fence. More rocks follow, one or two striking my back. I ignore the sting. It's temporary.

I'm almost to the fence when my left temple explodes in blinding pain. I stumble, disoriented. The world spins around me in sickening circles until my legs buckle, and I crash to the ground. I can barely hear the shouts and heavy footfalls approaching over the thunderous pounding in my head. I only have seconds to react before they're on me.

I latch onto the first man, using him to drag myself upright. After tossing him over the fence, I start to turn back, but something solid connects with my head. The world goes black as I fall.

When I come to, I find myself staring up at a darkening sky. The moon has already risen, glowing like a faint orb in the distance. I glance around, taking in my precarious situation. Ropes at my wrists and ankles have me staked down at the crossroads. How very fitting. Seven thousand years of life comes down to a well-thrown rock and old folk traditions about the strigoi. I'm sure my brother would find this a fitting consequence of my actions.

"You must stake the correct heart. The one that pumps the life-blood," a villager nearby says.

I've always wondered where that particular belief originated. I don't have two hearts and I wasn't infected with vampirism. I was born this way, although, the need for blood didn't kick in until I was about fifteen years old…millenniums ago.

The peasants argue back and forth while I stretch my neck. A splitting headache still roars inside my skull, but at least the world isn't spinning now.

"No, if your strike is not true, he will kill us all!"

It's a rather fair point. I twist my wrists, testing the rope. There's some give, but not quite enough to work my hands free.

"The strigoi is awake!" A woman shrieks somewhere behind me.

The two arguing men swing their fearful gaze to me, and I can't help but antagonize them. After opening my mouth wide, the deadly fangs unfold to extend past my teeth, and I hiss. Uninspired and dramatic perhaps, but the men jump back several steps, clutching their wooden stakes.

"Release me, and I won't slaughter you," I lie.

The men hesitate and exchange a considering look. Hmm. I didn't expect the tactic to work, but perhaps—

"No!" The woman yells adamantly. "They are liars! You must stake the heart and remove the head."

Well, that sounds less than desirable. The stake alone can end me. Decapitation seems a bit…excessive.

The two men clutch their stakes tighter and take a step toward me. I pull at the ropes binding my wrists, the rough material biting into my skin. I bare my fangs again, hoping to scare them off, but they only pause for a moment this time. Their grim faces are set…determined, thanks to the hysterical hag. Fuck.

"Kill the stigoi!" More voices chant.

I glance down the length of my body to see six people, one of whom carries the child I killed. Well, I can't say I didn't provide them motivation. Still, the thought of mere humans ending my long life, burns in my very viscera.

The two men draw closer, intent stares locked on my bared chest. It seems they intend to stake both of my supposed hearts at the same time. The chant grows louder, overpowering the vicious throbbing in my skull.

"Stop!" The sharp command cuts through the moment like a knife. The men halt, their gaze swinging to the now silent villagers, who are peering behind them.

The group splits, making way for someone.

"I am Dragaica, the Lady of Flowers," a feminine voice calls out with stern authority.

The villagers bow their heads and part further, allowing the newcomer more room. I stare down the line of my body to see a woman in their midst. At least…I think it's a woman.

Moonlight glows against her pale skin and sheer crimson wraps around her delicate form, held in place only by golden clasps and bands. A Mongol sword rests in her hand. She holds it loosely at her side. I'm struck by the creature's ethereal beauty and the thick curls of her raven-black hair. It must be the head injury.

I've never found a human woman enticing, at least not after my first forty years. The pitiful creatures quickly lost their appeal. Blood has been my only constant…the one thing that arouses any of my senses.

"Cut him loose," the strange woman commands in slow, firm words.

One of the villagers, a younger woman, falls to her knees. "Dragaica, my lady, he is a strigoi!" she pleads.

The mysterious woman turns, her gaze falling on me. "All creatures of the dark *belong to me!*"

The odd declaration takes me by surprise at first, but then the anger sets in. *I belong to no one and nothing.*

As this *Dragaica* saunters closer, moonlight glinting off the gold bands, the young villager grabs at her skirt.

"No! You mustn't! He will kill you, my lady!"

The clearly delusional stranger halts and turns toward the young woman, extending her hand. The villager clasps it in both of hers.

"Oh, thank you, Dragaica. Thank you for your bless…" The words trail off until they're no longer audible. The kneeling woman begins to pale and then collapses backward. Her lifeless eyes stare back at me, sparking an obsessive curiosity.

My gaze snaps back up to Dragaica and a slight smile curves her full lips before her impassive stare turns back to me. "Release him now or you shall all suffer her fate."

No one moves or makes a single sound. They all stare in shock at the young woman's still form.

"Release the strigoi!" Dragaica practically growls the words as she snatches the throat of the man closest to her. He fights against her, hitting and slapping at her arm, but she doesn't flinch. Her grip only grows tighter, and I watch in rapt fascination as his movements slow…his skin pales…his breath hitches.

This is no mere woman.

Two of the men attack, but she releases the dead man, and deftly evades the others' clumsy blows. Before they recover their balance, she digs her nails into the forearm of each man. I watch the life bleed from them without a single wound.

A third man rushes her, but her hand grips his throat and stops him momentum with surprising strength. This one she pulls closer, whispering something to him I can't hear.

A breeze makes the shimmering red fabric billow as she lets his dead body fall to the ground, and I am in awe.

7. Savagery

Luminita

The three remaining villagers move quickly now. While they busy themselves with untying the strigoi, I back up a few steps, but keep my eyes on *him*. The jolt of anger when I claimed all creatures of the night belong to me was…amusing. However, the reverence he exuded when I ripped the emotional souls from the men at my feet…that was rather intoxicating.

The strigoi's grey eyes track my every movement, ignoring the peasants who cut at his bindings. When the last rope falls to the ground, his attention shifts. He snatches the man who still holds a stake, and his eyes cut back to me for an instant, assessing, before he buries his teeth in the man's neck. Shrieks fill the air, and the remaining villagers scatter like insects.

To my surprise, the strigoi doesn't drink from the man. Instead, he viciously tears through his throat, removing a chunk of flesh, and spits it to the ground with disdain. Blood sprays the creature's face in fast, rhythmic spurts, but he meets my gaze again with a fearsome intensity.

An eager grin stretches my lips as I toss the sword toward him. It skids on the packed dirt. His gaze follows the blade until it stops in front of him. Then his attention returns to me inquisitively.

"Prove your worth, *Sălbatic.*"

Jenny Allen

Something shifts in the creature's grey eyes, and an odd hunger floods the air. He grabs the sword as he stands, keeping his gaze on me with a burning curiosity. For a moment, we simply stare at each other. I can feel the challenge and indignation roiling beneath his skin. There is a strong dislike for following orders, but he's intrigued.

Suddenly, he turns, and tears off in the direction of the fleeing peasants. They are running toward the forest, hoping to escape, but I doubt he'll allow that. And if he does...I will not.

After a few moments, the strigoi returns clutching a screaming woman. She wears a bite mark on her neck, but he didn't tear through her throat as he did the first man. How disappointing. Perhaps he is not the savage I thought he was.

The strigoi tosses the old woman into the dirt with a sneer. She sniffles and weeps like a pathetic little thing. The creature is unmoved by her tears. He raises the sword, and I stare in wonder as he cleaves off each limb without pause. The shrieks start to die off as the woman's shock settles in. She sobs, and he struts around her decimated body, staring viciously at what remains of her.

"You wanted them to cut off my head," he says in a growling voice that sends a shiver over my skin.

"No," the old woman pleads weakly.

The strigoi does not hesitate. He brings the blade down against her neck, but not with the same power he exerted on her arms and legs. The blade stops halfway through, and a malicious smile curves his lips. The act was purposeful. He wants to deny her a clean death...to enjoy her suffering.

He intently studies each gargling, choking breath that rattles from the woman's chest until they eventually cease. The creature's fixation doesn't stop until he places a boot on her bloody chest and roughly pulls the sword from her neck. Still, he stands there—broad chest heaving, covered in crimson, grip tightening on the sword—and watches the blood soak the ground.

After a moment, his gaze shifts back to the forest...to where the last man disappeared. He storms off in that direction like a wrathful god...like Ares himself. The strigoi revels in the blood and violence just as the Roman god from myth. Perhaps this world still contains some mysteries worth solving after all.

When he returns, dragging the last villager behind him, my grin widens. Not only does he relish this…he wants to see if I do as well. He could have killed them both when he caught them. Instead, he has brought them here…for me to bear witness to his darkness.

This time, he severs the man's hands before kneeling behind the squealing human. Despite the sword's sharp edge, he grips the blade in one hand, the pommel in the other, and brings it to the man's throat. The human goes still, but the savage's eyes raise to meet mine defiantly. He continues to study me as he tugs the sword back into the man's throat.

I ignore the gushing blood and choking sounds, content to hold the strigoi's challenging stare. Even as he backs up, allowing the villager to fall to the ground, he doesn't break eye contact. The creature rises slowly, grips the sword, and yanks it free. Then and only then, does his gaze leave mine. With one powerful strike, he severs the man's head. But his show isn't complete.

The savage bends, his fingers digging into the dead man's hair, and he raises the severed head above his to drink the blood dripping from it. It's barbaric…primal…and reverent, as if drinking a holy sacrament…a sacred toast to his god-like violence. I observe every nuance, soak in every riotous emotion from him, and a deep hunger springs to life inside me.

Sălbatic. It is a fitting name.

The strigoi discards the severed head, and his heated stare collides with mine. In that moment, it nearly steals my breath. With purposeful strides, he marches up to me, stopping inches away, and his eyes narrow.

"I am no one's to command," he states firmly, but I can sense the confliction in him…the obsessive curiosity.

"Only mine."

The sword clangs to the ground and his bloody hand snatches my throat firmly. "No one's," he repeats in guttural tones.

I glare into his pale grey eyes and grip his wrist. I don't want to hurt the creature. He's far too intriguing, but a point must be made. I squeeze, knowing my unexpected strength will surprise him. His brow furrows, and he attempts to pull away from me. I don't allow him.

While gently tugging at his rather unique energy, I take a step closer.

"What are you?" he asks, still conflicted. His burning need to know wars with his independence and a tiny sprig of fear enters his signature. A delectable combination.

I ignore the question and rise on my tiptoes to whisper, invading his space. "*Mine* to command. *Sălbatic meu.*" With one quick tug at his emotional soul, his hand falls from neck, his legs buckle, and he sinks to his knees.

A shocked expression lights his blood-soaked face as it tilts up toward me. "Who are you?" he asks in a breathy whisper full of awe.

A delicious smile graces my lips as I lean close. My fingers delve into his bloody hair with an almost soothing caress, and I whisper near his ear. "I am Luminita Dragomir…eater of souls, and you *Sălbatic meu*, are mine to command."

When I pull back, his stare narrows at me, but he does not argue this time.

"And who are you, *Sălbatic meu?*"

"I have had many names." The vague answer amuses me, but I arch a brow and hold his stare firmly. "Some have called me Enmesarra, vampire, strigoi…but Aaron is the name I've chosen."

My head tilts to the side as I consider him, and my raven curls spill over my shoulder. Aaron's gaze shifts to my hair only for a moment, but the desire surging through him is undeniable, and it lingers far after his eyes return to mine.

"I think Sălbatic suits you better," I say with a wicked grin.

8. Eater of Souls

Aaron

As we walk through the forest, I stay a step behind Luminita, not because I'm subservient, but to watch her. The deadly creature holds my fascination. The moonlight cutting through the canopy of young leaves illuminates her seemingly delicate form beneath the shimmering red fabric. It glints off the golden bands at her neck, arms, and waist and makes her creamy skin glow. Although she does look ethereal and otherworldly, she doesn't present as a predator. There is no outward hint of her physical strength or strange abilities. Yet somehow...this petite thing brought me to my knees...*me*...a veritable god who has spent seven thousand years as the pinnacle of conscious life.

I've come across other unusual creatures. Ahhazu was the first. She was an Akkadian of perfect health, but a deadly sickness travelled in her wake. It did not affect me or my brothers, of course, but many humans died. There were others—A witch of some repute among the Slavs called Baba Yaga, a small group of odd creatures in Ireland who prefer to eat children, an Erinyes in Greece with a wicked mind for vengeance, the secretive group of Gigantes nestled in the Roman hills, the Androphagi who consume human flesh, and Shamans who can send their spirit out of their bodies. I've even heard rumors of shifters among the various cultures…people who can alter their form…impersonate animals. I've never set eyes on one, however.

Tales of demons, seductresses, and succubus are pervasive through every culture, but I've never found any truth to them. Most often, I am disappointed to find a woman who is considered beautiful pulling the strings of lesser men. They may worship these women, but they're mere humans and their physical beauty quickly fades. None of the supposed demons had any power beyond the ability to harden a man's cock. Human males are such vulnerable creatures, especially where sex is concerned.

When we enter a clearing in the trees, my eyes shift to the pack she carries. The blanket and silk cord seem…familiar for some reason. It nags at me until I recall the unusual hut…the one I camped out in until Timisoara was safe. I'd wrapped that same blanket around my shoulders while watching the burning city.

"You are from Timisoara," I say plainly, breaking the long silence.

Luminita stops and peers over her shoulder at me. In the light of the full moon, her sea-colored eyes almost glow. "You stayed in my home." It wasn't a question, but a statement of fact.

"How do you know that?" My eyes narrow in suspicion. I'd searched the immediate area in hopes of finding the hut's owner before I left for Timisoara. She couldn't know with certainty that I was the one in her hut. Perhaps she is only guessing based on my statement but wants to appear assertive.

The woman considers me for a few silent seconds before a wicked smile crosses her full lips. "I sensed your hunger. That's how I found you."

My brow wrinkles at that, but before I open my mouth, she turns and continues across the clearing. I catch up in a few strides, and pace beside her. "My hunger?"

"Yes," she says, still facing the path before her. "It's very old… unique."

"And you are no mere human."

The woman glances at me with a sly grin. "Obviously not."

"Then what are you?"

"I already told you, Sălbatic. An eater of souls."

Irritation itches my skin. "That is myth. There are no souls. I've lived long enough to know that truth."

Luminita comes to a sudden stop, and I halt with her. Slowly, she turns and stares up at me, searching my eyes. "How long?"

The audacity of the question plucks a nerve. She is unwilling to truthfully give me answers, yet demands them from me? "Long enough," I repeat defiantly.

She takes a step closer, but her gaze falls to my shirt, now stiff with dried blood. When her eyes finally rise to meet mine again, they hold the same coldness I witnessed when she killed the villagers. "How long?" she repeats in a threatening tone.

When I merely stare at her in amusement, she grips my arm, nails digging into the fabric.

"Do you require another demonstration?"

"How does it work?"

Her eyes narrow to sharp points. "You claim there is no soul, but yet you feel."

The odd statement takes me by surprise, but she continues.

"Right now, you are shocked, curious, and..." The corner of her full lips lift. "Aroused."

I lift one eyebrow with an amused huff. "An interesting guess, though the first two are fairly evident."

When her tongue wets her lips and she flashes a devious grin, it stirs something long dormant in me.

"Perhaps aroused is an understatement." Her laugh is almost melodic. "And it is no guess, Sălbatic. I sense your emotions as if they are my own. It's what I feed on, what sustains me..." A malicious glint fills her eyes. "...what I ripped from those villagers. That is the soul I consume."

A sudden wave of weakness strikes me like it had in the village, but I stay on my feet this time.

"I can take a little...or...everything. Now...how long have you lived, Sălbatic?"

Jenny Allen

After eyeing her for a moment, I relent. There is no harm in answering the odd creature's question. "My first memories are of Sumer, although after so many years, it is difficult to recall if that is where I originated."

The surprise on her moonlit face is rather exquisite.

"And you, *Dragaica*?" I lean in, my curiosity drawing me closer until I crowd her vision. "Where did you come from, Lady of Flowers?" The sight of her dark pupils expanding brings a smile to my face. I'm not the only one aroused, apparently.

Still, she fiercely holds my stare. "I was born near the Bay of Kotor nearly three hundred years ago."

The confession rips through me. Three hundred years. Although it is still a mere moment in my lifespan, it's far longer than any non-vampire creature I've come across. *If* she speaks the truth, that is.

I sink my hand into her soft raven-black curls and hover closer until our breath mingles. "Truth?"

Her nails dig into my arm and I'm suddenly on my knees again. Luminita stands over me like a vengeful goddess bathed in ethereal light. "You do not have permission to touch me." The sharp tones are unforgiving.

Anger surges to the surface as I glare up at her divine beauty. The creature's abilities are infuriating. Thousands of years as the deadliest thing to prowl the land and this delicate being has me at her mercy.

"Retract them or I'll end you."

At first, I'm confused by her command. Then I feel the prick of my fangs against my bottom lip. I wasn't even aware they'd unfolded. I do as she directs because I refuse to let this be the way I die. I don't believe in souls, but the woman has some sort of power…some ability to weaken me like the villagers she killed.

Luminita sternly holds my gaze and leans closer. "I am no man's property. I chose my own path. You will *not* touch me again without invitation. Am I understood?"

The words summon my defiance once more, and she releases my arm to grip my throat with crushing strength.

"I do not wish to kill you, Sălbatic. You are the first interesting thing I've come across. But if you refuse to follow my rules, you will leave me little choice." Her fingers squeeze until I can't drag in a single breath past her grip.

Fire ignites in my lungs and the world begins to spin. With a rough nod, she releases me, and I choke on the cool night air. I double over, dragging in deep breaths between the coughs. When the fit finally stops, I sit back on my heels, panting.

"We have an understanding then?"

Every fiber of my being rebels against the notion. I have never taken orders from another. *Ever.* Much to my brother's dismay, I might add. However, this creature...this eater of souls...has me at a disadvantage.

Fingers drift into my blood-matted hair and tighten sharply. "I can taste your defiance." Luminita moves nearer to whisper, and her closeness causes a different emotion to overthrow my anger. Her breath washes over the shell of my ear, and I swallow hard on the overwhelming desire it summons. "Follow me, Sălbatic, and I'll whisper my secrets while we tear a bloody path through the world."

When she pulls back to meet my eyes, wicked delight curves those plump lips, and I've *never*...in all my years...wanted someone the way I do now.

9. The River

Luminita

The raw, aching desire pulsating beneath the man's skin is exhilarating. I've sensed the lewd cravings of men before, but this…is different…more…ancient. It calls to me, but the Durand do not give into their emotions. *I* do not give in.

As his ravenous gaze lingers on my lips, my grin fades, and I release his hair. The sudden sense of loss he feels startles me as much as his yearning. I turn away from him and continue through the trees. Judging by the clear rippling sounds, the river is not far now.

In seconds, he is once again matching my stride, and I feel his burning curiosity like a physical touch. Thankfully, he doesn't speak.

While we continue through the woods, I stuff down the unsettling urges this man seems to elicit. Enjoyment is one thing, but control must be maintained, especially with a creature as deadly as this one. I cannot afford to relinquish even a hint of authority and allowing him to satisfy my lust would do just that.

When the river is finally in sight, Sălbatic breaks the odd silence. "Before…you said that's how you found me. What did you mean?"

I say nothing, and his frustration grows.

"This is not a word I typically use, but…please."

The effort sounds painful, which makes me smile, if only briefly. "All of my kind sense emotion, but I am…different. When a feeling is strong enough, it leaves an impression behind…a trail. Your hunger is ancient, potent, almost palpable. That is how I tracked you."

"You *tracked* me? Sought me out?" Both his signature and his voice betray his surprise, which I find odd.

How else would I have found him?

"Why?"

"I thought I already made that quite obvious."

"Why?" He repeats a little firmer.

"Outside of my kind, I have not come across another creature like myself. I left my family some time ago. Women are not granted positions of power among them. We are nothing more than possessions to be traded." I try not to let the bitter disgust leak into my voice, but it is an old wound. "I've lived among humans for too long. Their lives are short, pointless, and…depressing, honestly. The idea of uncovering something new was far too tempting to resist, so I followed your trail from Timisoara."

"So, there are more…like you?"

"*Da.*"

"If that's true, why have I not met one before now?" Suspicion clings to his words, as if he still doubts me.

"You most likely have, if I am to believe *your* claims. In seven thousand years, you must have. But we are a close-knit, highly secretive race. We do not reveal ourselves to outsiders."

"Like you are now?"

I take note of the humor in his words. It is a fair point. "As I said before, I am…different. Unlike my family, I understand the benefit of a powerful ally."

"Is that what I am? An ally?"

We break through the forest's edge, and I stop to scan the area. A small river cuts through the rocky field. Big enough to bathe in at least. When I turn toward him, he's staring at me expectantly.

"Are you my enemy?" I ask plainly while setting down my pack.

Sălbatic considers me for a moment before shaking his head. "No."

Draga & the Savage: Dragobete

"Then are we not potential allies?" I kick off my little leather shoes.

"I thought I was *yours to command?*" The aggravation in his gravelly voice does not go unnoticed. "That does not sound like an ally."

I turn away from him to face the river while I unhook the fabric from the band circling my neck. "Working in unison takes trust and dedication, Sălbatic." That same insatiable desire roars to life at my back and I take a step closer to the river. "It requires time for those bonds to form." I unclasp the golden belt and the crimson fabric floats to the ground. "Until then…" I peer over my shoulder and drink in the sight of his obvious arousal. He hasn't taken a single step toward me. The man stands, rigid as stone, hands clenched at his sides, but his eyes blaze. "You *are* mine to command. Prove your worth."

I step down into the knee-high river, the chilling water rushing around my bare legs, cooling my heated skin.

"And if I leave?"

The unexpected question gives me pause, and I hold his hungry gaze. "Are you?"

A muscle twitches in his cheek as his jaw clenches tight. Even without my abilities, the confliction within him is clear.

I avert my gaze to the river, bending to scoop up a handful of water. "You are free to leave if you wish, Sălbatic. I will grant you that, at least."

He says nothing as I splash the crisp water over my skin, but I know he hasn't moved from that spot.

I crouch down and use handfuls from the river to wet my hair. "If you decide to stay, I suggest bathing."

"Suggest or command?" he finally says.

I peer at him between the wet strands of my hair with an amused grin. "Do you require a command to bathe? Perhaps I have chosen poorly."

The words only stoke his anger, which I quite enjoy. Despite that, he moves toward the bank, pulling the bloody shirt over his head. Even through the blood caking his skin, I can see the light smattering of dark hair covering his broad chest. Tension pulls at every deliciously cut muscle as if the very act of complying is painful to him. Perhaps I shouldn't derive pleasure from that, but he is quite the specimen.

He keeps his heated gaze firmly fixed on me as he tugs off each boot and allows them to fall. When his hands move to his belt, his demeanor shifts. The anger sinks into the background, and that salacious hunger resurfaces.

I don't look away. Doing so would imply he has some power over me. Instead, I watch in calm indifference as he tugs away the leather belt, pulls down his blood-stained *cioareci,* and removes his woolen socks. Sălbatic is an impressive creature in *many* aspects, though I don't permit him to see my interest.

I return to combing my wet fingers through my hair and shift my attention to the horizon where the sky lightens, heralding the dawn. Feet splash into the water nearby, but he doesn't approach me.

"You should wash your garments as well. Once they've dried, we can follow the river to the next town, and find you more…suitable clothing."

Water sloshes behind me, but he maintains his distance. I wonder if he does so because he fears me or his own desires. Perhaps it is both.

When I rise to my feet, cold water sluicing down my legs, his splashing stops. I peek over to see him watching me once more. His dark hair is slicked back and reddened water drips down his chest. The growing sunlight reveals deep lines bracketing his mouth with his slight smile. An impressive specimen indeed.

I turn my focus to my pack and saunter out of the river. The splashing doesn't resume until I unfasten the silk cords, remove the blanket, and wrap it around myself. An amused smile tugs at my lips.

The sun begins to slip free of the horizon, but the trees block its early rays, so I move closer to the riverbank. When I reach a spot in the weak sunlight, I spread the blanket across the ground and lie down. Eventually, the sun will warm my chilled skin and I could use the rest. It will take time for his clothes to dry, and this spot seems untouched by civilization.

I don't hear Sălbatic leave the water for quite some time, but then blood is not easy to clean from wool. Impossible, actually. At the very least, his clothes will maintain a pinkish brown color.

"Are you sleeping…here…in the open…naked?" The voice comes from my right, close, but not too close.

I crack one eye open and stare up at his nude form hovering beside the blanket. "I'm cold. The sun will warm me."

"There are…other ways to stay warm."

For some reason, his growling words make my thighs clench. The proposal is obvious, but it's his tone or perhaps the man himself that affects me, which is…disturbing.

I lean up on my elbows and meet his heated stare. "Perhaps you're right. I'm dry enough for clothes."

Something hardens in his eyes and that delicious surge of frustration fills the air again.

"Hand me my shift?" I politely request with a pleasant smile.

His hands curl into fists again but not from a need for violence. He desperately wants to touch me but knows I won't allow it. And at least for now, he is not willing to risk my wrath.

"Please." I grant him that one small mercy.

A growl rumbles from his throat, but he turns and stalks toward my clothes. While his back is turned, I admire the rather enticing view, but once he retrieves my long white shift, I avert my gaze and lie back down.

When he returns, he clears his throat to capture my attention.

"Thank you, Sălbatic." I take the garment from him as I sit up, but he only stares at me. I slip the shift over my head and tug it down until it covers my thighs. Although the fabric is not sheer like my dress, it is thin. At least it's some sort of barrier, although the heat in his eyes has not wavered. He still watches me ravenously.

I scoot to the blanket's edge and curl onto my side, facing away from him. "You may lie down if you wish."

The man hesitates, but after a moment, I feel his warmth behind me.

"You are an infuriating creature," he whispers in a deep voice, but the words hold no malice.

A grin cracks my lips. "Most men are not accustomed to a strong woman."

"You are *no mere woman*." The statement is almost reverent.

"Obviously not."

10. Madness

Aaron

When Luminita's breathing falls into a slow, steady rhythm, I sit up to stare at her slumbering face. She is honestly asleep. She's seen the things I've done, the brutality I'm capable of, and yet she fell asleep with her back to me. I'm uncertain if I'm more in awe of that fact or angered by it. Is it possible that even after my savage display, she doesn't consider me a threat? Or is she simply certain in her power over me?

I shift and allow my hand to hover over her shoulder, close enough to feel the heat of her skin through the fabric. Her eyes move rapidly behind her lids and a small sound escapes her lips, but she doesn't wake. I could do whatever I desire in this vulnerable moment. The knowledge reawakens the lustful thoughts she summoned earlier. I watch my hand as it drifts down the line of her ribs without touching…the swell of her hip…the curve of her shapely ass and every inch hardens my already throbbing cock.

It must be her power, her inhumanness that draws me. I've seen women in all shapes and forms, even ones similar to hers, and none of them has called to me in such a primal, carnal way. I don't even recall the last time my body reacted to a woman's touch, much less the mere sight of one.

Perhaps it is the possibility of more than fleeting physical gratification. According to her claims, she's lived three hundred years and still appears youthful. Or perhaps I'm intrigued by the power she wields so acutely, her vicious nature mirroring my own, or the keen intellect she obviously possesses.

My hand drops to the blanket as I realize the dangerous little creature is correct in her assumption. I won't harm her. Never like this. She is the first truly worthy opponent I have encountered and the thought of dispatching her in a cowardly moment such as this offends me.

I could leave...walk away right now, but I won't do that either. If she was honest about her gifts, she could simply track me again. Part of me is tempted to test her ability, but the thought she might not want to seek me out a second time stops me. The simple truth is I want her...beyond reason, beyond thought.

Follow me, Sălbatic, and I'll whisper my secrets while we tear a bloody path through the world. The words she whispered in my ear, a violent promise, set me aflame. If not for her rule about being touched and her infuriating ability to enforce it, I would have thrown her down in the woods right there and ravaged every inch of her fragile-looking form. The nearly overwhelming compulsion almost drove me to it regardless.

A low growl vibrates in my throat as I push to my feet and stalk toward my damp clothes. The need to touch her soft skin...to plunge inside her heat and be lost...tears at me despite the release I granted myself in the river earlier. I can't recall the last time I felt the desire to even stroke myself. The creature is madness incarnate...a Dionysian frenzy in woman form.

As I grab the wet *cioareci*, a thought occurs to me. If Luminita is capable of sensing others' emotions, feeding off them, can she implant them as well? And if so, could she accomplish that while asleep? I pull on the wool pants, hoping the chill will ease the hardness that desperately desires her. The cold is jolting at first but does little to solve my dilemma. I pull on the stained linen shirt as well, welcoming the cold bite of the fabric against my heated skin, though it only lasts a moment.

My gaze drifts to the river and then back to Luminita's still-sleeping form. Although I would welcome sleep after such an eventful night, I know I won't find it beside her. At least, not until I quell the ravenous beast coiling around my insides, *if* such a thing is even possible.

After wading into the river, sitting in the chilly waters, and succumbing to the urge for a second release, I finally venture back to the blanket. I don't lie down on it, however. My clothes are still sopping wet, so I pace around her and lie down on the grass in front of her.

I watch her sleep for some time, taking in every detail from the way her drying hair curls over her shoulder to the dark lashes resting against her cheeks to her slightly parted lips. I force my eyes closed with a groan and will my blood to rush *anywhere* else than its current destination. When the pressure finally eases to a tolerable level, the exertion pulls me under, and I sleep.

When I eventually wake, the sun has moved beyond the halfway point in the sky. My head turns and my brow immediately furrows. The space beside me is empty. For one insane moment, I wonder if it was all some feverish dream. Then I hear footsteps on the grass and tilt my head back to peer behind me. Luminita is crouched before her pack, tying the silk cords. A black vest covers the top of her shift, and a thick braid spills over her shoulder as she works. The infuriating and unrelenting attraction is instantaneous.

I relax against the grass and gaze up at the blue sky dotted with clouds, trying to think about anything other than the woman driving me to madness.

"Tomorrow is Dragobete," she says as if sensing I'm awake. Then it occurs to me. That's precisely what happened.

"The Spring festival? It means something to you?" I ask inquisitively. I'm aware of the human celebration, though I never bothered to learn its intricacies.

"Rituals hold power, Sălbatic. Have you not learned that by now? Certainly, you've had ample opportunity in your long life." Luminita's voice moves closer as she speaks until she hovers in my field of vision with a curious smile.

"Some. Yes. Though I've found most to be hollow and pointless."

The expression on her face changes as if I've somehow presented her with a challenge. "And you believe the rituals of Dragobete are among the latter?"

I stare at her startling blue-green eyes. They'd been luminous in the dark, befitting of her name. But in the sunlight, they are hypnotic. "I've never cared about the festival enough to learn its rituals, to be honest. Is it not just another celebration of winter's end and the fertility of life?" I ask in a rather bored tone. The fact that such a powerful creature could find interest in a mundane thing such as this is unsettling.

"That would be *Mărțișor*," she chides. "Dragobete is a celebration of physical love."

That piques my interest and an odd sort of hope swells in my chest. "And you wish to indulge these traditions? With me?" I can't stop the grin spreading across my face.

One of Luminita's eyebrows lift before she wanders away from me. "I admit...I am rather curious if a creature of your strength will enhance the ritual," she says casually.

I sit up, watching her retrieve her pack, but she doesn't meet my eyes again. "What does this *ritual* include?"

"Burning herbs, wine with special ingredients..." she lists in a nonchalant tone before adding "...blood and sex magic."

I push to my feet and stride over to her, but she avoids meeting my suspicious stare. "If those were part of Dragobete, I'm certain I would have known about them."

After drawing in a deep breath, she finally meets my eyes again. "My kind's traditions vary somewhat from the human ones."

My head tilts, inviting her to elaborate, but she doesn't.

"You should finish dressing so we can be on our way." She hauls the light pack onto her shoulders and meets my stare with no sign of discomfort.

"What is the purpose of your ritual?" I ask, refusing to simply drop the subject.

"Should we head east or west along the river?" Her heads swings in both directions. "Perhaps west...away from the mountains?"

Draga & the Savage: Dragobete

I take a step closer but stop myself before I make the mistake of gripping her arm. "West. The Horde continued east along the Mureş River, and there is a town a short way from here. Now, what *precisely* is the purpose of this ritual of yours?"

The woman's lips press together in a firm line as she holds my insistent glare. Her fiery nature only inflames my desire and the visage of her...uncomfortable amuses me to no end.

I lean down to hover with a spreading grin. "I thought you intended to whisper your secrets to me. Do I need to come closer?"

Her glare hardens but she doesn't withdraw. "Pain is especially potent for my people, and sex is one of the few ways to draw from a person without risking their life. The correct combination with the right circumstances is believed to increase our power."

"Only on Dragobete?"

Her tongue wets her lips at my dark tone, but Luminita's steely resolve doesn't break. She doesn't close the distance between us. "*Especially* on Dragobete." Without another word, she steps around me and starts west along the river, leaving me to tug on my socks and boots.

11. Intense Fascination

Luminita

The walk along the river passes in silence for quite some time. I still feel his hungry gaze on me, however. His desire has only intensified since we arrived at the river, unsurprisingly. I fight back a smile at that thought. I'm not unaccustomed to being lusted after…wanted. Human males are rather eager creatures, but Sălbatic—or Aaron as he chooses to be called —is not some simple-minded farmer or youthful warrior.

He's lived thousands of lifetimes and most likely seen more than even I can comprehend. Yet, there is an odd sort of frenzy to his craving for me, as if it's an unfamiliar emotion he is ill equipped to handle. Drawing that out of an ancient creature such as him is both thrilling and alarming.

Perhaps I should not test his control but flirting that dangerous line… watching such a powerful specimen force himself *not* to act…controlling his response to me…might be my drug of choice. Although I was exhausted, I'm a rather light sleeper. I felt his hand hover over my form…close but never touching. I sensed his spiraling lust dragging him toward frenzy, testing his control, but he complied with my demands. He never crossed that line and didn't walk away either, despite having every opportunity to, or at least he thought so.

Had he chosen to leave, I would have merely tracked him again. Sălbatic is too rare a thing, and I still understand so little about him.

Besides, the thought of incorporating him into my Dragobete ritual swims through my veins like the finest opium.

Individually, humans are inconsequential, but in great numbers they are deadly. Should they eventually discover us and rise up in rebellion, amassing more power is the best way to avoid their collective wrath. I have always known the Durand are capable of so much more.

My family never considered my ideas valid. They walked through the rituals without enthusiasm, never investing in their power, content to simply exist as they always had. My father, in particular, often chided me for being zealous…for wanting to contaminate our holy race…for defying the gods that created us by seeking more than they'd deemed worthy of us. Dragomir had always been a short-sighted fool. The manner of his death only proved that.

I steal a glance at my companion who has finally dragged his stare away from me. The linen shirt and wool pants that were once a creamy white are rust-colored, and now that his hair has dried, the sun highlights subtle streaks of grey I hadn't noticed. The man exudes strength, even in the way he stalks beside me. He is the perfect specimen to further my ritual. Although…the effect he has on me…the way he's made my thighs clench and my pulse quicken…means I must take certain precautions. Maintaining control is critical.

Sălbatic seemed more than eager to partake in my Dragobete ritual. Of course, had I gone into greater detail, he might not be so excited by the concept. All things in good time. I need a few more ingredients for the brew before elaborating further. Hopefully, I can find them in town. I have most of them, but certain herbs are…difficult to procure. Datura seeds, *Măselariţa,* and *Mătrăguna* are a challenge to find this time of year.

As if reading my thoughts, Sălbatic finally breaks the silence. "Tell me more about this ritual of yours."

I eye him warily. Perhaps the creature has some sort of ability he hasn't disclosed. Although, if that had been the case, I surely would have seen prior evidence of it. "It requires an isolated place in the woods, a fire, a mixture of herbs to be burned, a wine infused with special herbs, a blood sacrifice, and a union in true Dionysian fashion." I list each element plainly, hoping it will satisfy his curiosity. Of course, it does not.

"What sort of blood sacrifice?"

The question inspires one of my own. "Are the legends true? Do you need to drink the blood of your victims or is that merely an indulgence?"

When he doesn't answer, I peer up at him. He watches me with hooded eyes while we walk. "Some is required every two or three days at least," he finally answers.

"And what happens if you do not drink what is required?"

The skin around his eyes tighten, once again assessing me. "I find breathing difficult, my head aches, and it weakens me."

Supplying such an honest answer is yet another display of his desire to trust me, which I find particularly satisfying. "Hmm. Perhaps you require an alteration to my ritual. An additional sacrifice. Having you at peak strength would be optimal."

"Having me?" His brow arches with an almost lecherous grin.

I manage to stifle the smile threating to break through. "Did I not state a Dionysian union is required? Do I need to speak in simpler terms."

The spike of anger and indignation stretches my carefully crafted control, and a smile breaks free.

"I am quite aware of the Dionysian mysteries and Bacchanals. I spent quite some time in that region. If you are from the Adriatic Sea, how do you know of them?"

"My family does not originate from Kotor. They brought their rituals with them from Genoa after the Carthaginians destroyed the city in the Second Punic war about a thousand years ago. Most of our traditions are an amalgamation of the ancient Genoa festival and the Kotoran, though I have made modifications to incorporate the magic of my new home here. My ancestors celebrate *Euhoi Bacchoi*, which aligns with *Mărțișor* here in Romania. However, I find the spirit of Dragobete to better resemble my interpretation."

"How long ago did you leave Kotor?"

Once again, my gaze cuts over to him. "Why do you wish to know?"

He glances back at me for a moment. "You are a rather unusual creature, and I find myself…" He seems to search for a word, his eyes focused on the horizon. "…curious, which is not something I've experienced many times in my life."

"Curious? Is that what you call it?" A sly grin stretches my lips and his gaze returns, colliding with mine. Heat thrums between us like a physical force, and I am not as immune as I like to pretend.

"Intense fascination if you prefer." His grey eyes darken and that thrum between us intensifies. "I am not accustomed to this level of…" Once again, he searches for a word. "…desire."

The way *desire* leaves his lips vibrates through my core.

"Or *any level*, to be honest. At least, not in a *very* long time."

Sălbatic's confession should not have this effect on me. It should not make my chest tighten and my body ache erotically. I am *not* a possession, a thing to be coveted, a mere body to claim. I am above such notions.

"The ritual is not about satisfying your base urges, Sălbatic." I speak in clipped tones as my hardening stare returns to the river before us. "It is a rite meant to unlock power, a sacred liberation from the prison of this world's banality."

In a quick motion, he turns and steps into my path, forcing me to stop. As my gaze travels up to his rather handsome face, burning need emanates from him in almost suffocating waves. For a split-second, I am almost lost to the wild carnality in his grey eyes.

"That is why I find you so…" His gaze falls to my lips and the heat between us makes my head swim. "…devastatingly irresistible. Ask me to touch you." The demand sounds more like a plea, drowning in need, and I almost say yes.

His gaze returns to my eyes, searching, when I do not answer. My heart pounds violently against my ribs, and he seems to sense it. Satisfaction leaks into his signature, and the corner of his mouth lifts. It only hardens my resolve. Conceding now would equate defeat.

I take one step back while firmly holding his questioning stare. "No."

The man's broad chest heaves beneath his linen shirt while he glares at me. "Why not?"

"Because *I* am not *yours* to command," I state firmly.

Once again, his jaw clenches tight and his hands curl into fists as he fights the impulse to touch me regardless. His control is rather admirable, although, some deep part of me wishes he'd lose his grip and embrace his savage nature even with me.

"Dragaica, Luminita, Eater of Souls, please…allow me to touch you."

The request pulls me closer, and I consider consenting, but it would serve my purpose better to save such energy for the rite. "No," I respond slowly. I can feel the rising anger and frustration, which I typically enjoy, but for some reason it feels bittersweet in this moment.

"But…" I reach up, letting my fingertips drift over the rough stubble on his cheek. The shiver that courses through him at the simple touch, seeps into my skin. His eyes close as if he's savoring every nuance. "…soon, Sălbatic. Save your energy for Dragobete."

Before he opens his eyes, I withdraw my hand and walk around him, continuing toward our destination. "Is the town far?" I call over my shoulder when I don't hear his footsteps behind me.

Even from this distance, his rumbling growl of frustration vibrates over my skin.

12. Deva

Aaron

Deva is a larger city than I recall. It sprawls much farther across the river's side than the last time I was here. The tall hill rising from its midst is familiar, but not the partially built structure at its zenith—a fortress or a castle of some sort. The once sleepy town I knew as Decidava is now a veritable metropolis compared to Orăştie, the tiny village where I encountered Luminita.

My gaze lowers to the infuriating woman as she walks the streets in front of me, heading for the marketplace. The demoness seems to enjoy my torment far too much, tempting me with her bare flesh yet denying my touch.

Save your energy for Dragobete, she said. *Save my energy*…as if I'm some common mortal lacking in stamina. Although the words still burn in my gut like lava, the humiliation of asking permission and *still* being denied cuts far deeper. I have *never* used the word please in all my time, and now I have used the infernal word twice because of this devilish creature.

Unfortunately, the seductive sway of her hips is far too hypnotic. Resisting the urge to wrap my hands around them and pull her back against me is nearly overwhelming. The bustling people, the buildings, the noise, even the stench fades until she is the only thing that remains.

I wonder how much is caused by her power, or if it's simply the maddening allure of forbidden fruit.

Is this how humans feel desire? Do they live in this constant state of gut-churning frustration? Constantly suffer from yearning for something they may never have? If so, I understand now why they live such short lives. Surely, this hastens their deaths. I could not imagine surviving in this state for a millennium or more. A day has been excruciating enough.

I should walk away...return to the Mongol horde...continue my bloody tirade *without* this irritation...this unnecessary derailment from my existence...this unobtainable seductress...

Luminita stops, interrupting my raving thoughts. My eyes finally leave her to peer about the busy marketplace. The sun hangs low, casting everything in an orange hue. People hurry between stands and wagons, carrying bundles of various sizes. Children run rampant with ribbons fluttering in the breeze. The entire scene is rather exhausting and far too boisterous for my current mood.

When she peers over her shoulder and my gaze fixes to her sea-blue eyes, my earlier resolve to leave melts. I should walk away, but I won't. As exasperating as her games are, the creature is a mystery I cannot allow to go unsolved. She has burrowed into my mind and taken residence it seems, and my body is just as affected by her.

She considers me for a moment before moving closer, until I can feel the heat of her body. My traitorous heart quickens at her nearness. "Do you eat?" she whispers while people push past us.

"Yes. It is one of *many* annoying necessities." I try to keep my focus on her eyes, but still find my gaze drifting to her full lips. She's standing so close. It wouldn't take much to eliminate the distance between us...to take what I desire as I have always done. It is my divine right or has been for eons.

Luminita obviously senses my control becoming dangerously brittle and steps back while digging into the pocket of her vest. Then she holds out several gold denarii to me. "I need to find a few supplies for the rite. Can you procure some food and wine?"

Draga & the Savage: Dragobete

The anger and frustration that has been roiling beneath my skin since the moment she put me on my knees eases a touch. It is a request and not a command. "Anything in particular?"

"Food for travel, perhaps some grapes if you can find them. For the wine…" A faint smile crosses her face, far from innocent, but not quite wicked. Unfortunately, I find it exquisite. "…the more potent the better. Two bottles at least." Then something seems to occur to her, and she frowns up at me. "Does wine affect you differently?"

Someone bumps into my back, and I take a stumbling step forward. I narrowly avoid pinning Luminita to the wall, much to my relief and disappointment. "Why do you ask?" The growl in my voice is unavoidable when surrounded by so many people.

"If you are familiar with Bacchanal and the Dionysian Mysteries, then you know why." The fire in her challenging glare heats my skin. As much as it irritates me, I also find it arousing. Unlike these tiresome humans, she is not weak in body or mind.

"Altered consciousness…the frenzy?"

She nods.

"I am not immune to the effects of wine, although some substances are less effective." This seems to pique her interest.

"Such as…"

My eyes narrow, but before I can speak, another human crashes into me. Suddenly, Luminita's back is to the wall with my body firmly pressed against her delicious form. Everything stirs inside me at once. She is so soft yet unyielding.

"Sălbatic," she says in a soft voice.

My chest heaves with each quickened breath and I can already feel my arousal hardening against her. "Draga." The whispered word surprises me when it passes my lips. I'd intended to say Dragaica, seeing as that is the name she prefers among humans, but what emerged was something unexpected and far more damning.

Her eyes rake up my body to meet mine, and for a split second, I see the same raw ache mirrored in them. Then it's gone.

"Step away," she commands in firm tones. Anger lights her eyes now, but it seems hollow.

I know what I saw. Did my closeness cause her reaction, or was it the word I mistakenly whispered?

"Now, Sălbatic!"

I comply, but only because ravaging her here on the street would cause problems and the markets won't be open for much longer. Once I step back, Luminita's hands smooth her vest and shift, but there is a faint hint of color in her cheeks.

For some inexplicable reason, a sudden urge to ease her discomfort overcomes me. "*Măselariţa* ...it doesn't have much effect on me for some reason."

Luminita's gaze snaps to mine as if I've said something significant. "Are there any other herbs you are immune to?"

I study that calculating gaze of hers for a moment. Handing this creature further ammunition to control me is unwise. She hasn't revealed specific details of this *ritual*. What if I'm simply providing her with the means to end my long life? Of course, with her powers...her ability to consume life's essence, she doesn't require assistance from mere plants. If her intention was to harm me, she could easily accomplish that where we stand.

"Akonit. I believe some call it Wolfsbane."

The woman nods thoughtfully and then meets my eyes again, immediately stoking the heat that never seems to dissipate in her presence. "Thank you. For being honest."

The odd genuineness in her voice gives me pause and I lean down to whisper a little closer to her ear. "How do you know I'm being honest?" It might be the sun looming closer to the horizon, but it appears as if the creamy skin along her neck blushes faintly.

Luminita presses her palm into the center of my chest and pushes, forcing me to take a step back. The strength lurking in her fragile form still surprises me.

A familiar warning flashes in those sea-blue eyes. "How many times must I explain? I feel every flicker of emotion from you, Sălbatic. I know when you are conflicted, suspicious, and frustrated. I also know when you reach a resolution and *submit*."

The emphasis she places on the last word wipes the amusement from my face. *Submit?* The very idea offends me, but the accuracy of her statement grates along every single nerve. "Compliance is *not* submission, Dragaica."

She tilts her head up toward me with a knowing smile before slipping away. "Two bottles, Sălbatic." She calls over her shoulder as she disappears into the crowd.

Once I've procured most of the requested items, I search the market for the raven-haired creature. I find her amid a crowd of people and concern knits my brow at first. Humans may be insignificant and weak, but in numbers, they pose a threat, even to Luminita.

When I approach the gathered mass, however, there seems to be no animosity in the group. Quite the opposite. Luminita stands with people circled around her, holding the hand of a young man with her eyes closed.

"There is one you wish to approach with flowers tomorrow," she says in haunting tones.

"Yes, Dragaica," the boy replies with an edge of wonder.

"And she is here? Now?"

The boy scans the crowd and when his gaze stops, Luminita opens her eyes with a smile but doesn't follow his line of sight. "Yes, Dragaica. She is here."

Luminita turns and stares directly at the maidan, even though the boy averted his gaze and never singled her out. "She will accept your offering."

A brilliant smile lights the young man's face, and he quickly digs into his pocket. "Oh, thank you, Lady of Flowers!" He presses the gold coin into her palm before turning it to place a kiss on the back of her hand. "Thank you!" The boy retreats from the open space, and the gathered crowd erupts with pleas to be chosen next.

I place the basket of gathered goods at my feet and lean against a closed market stand. The red and pinks of the setting sun paint the scene in vivid colors as I watch her work through each request. The show is rather fascinating and obviously pays well. Some patrons request confirmation of their chosen ones for tomorrow's festival, some seek solace from dead relatives—I'm rather curious to know how she accomplishes that particular trick—and some wish to know if they are with child.

By the time she's granted each request, the sky is dark, torches light the square, and her pockets overflow with denarii. I wait in my chosen spot as she gathers her pack and scans the area. When her gaze lands on me, her faint smile inflames the constant hum of lust I've felt since the moment she drained the life from the young woman in Orăştie.

Luminita saunters closer, each movement like a fluid dance of seduction, or perhaps that's merely my perception. I bend to gather the basket of goods, distracting myself from her lithe form for a moment.

"There were no grapes," I state, taking my time before straightening to my full height again. "Too early in the season."

"A pity, but we can make do. The innkeeper has gifted us a room for the night in exchange for her reading."

The simple statement should not quicken my breath, but it does. The woman's relentless effect on me is beyond unnerving. "How very practical of you."

A seemingly genuine smile stretches her full lips before she turns and begins walking. I follow, of course. At this point, I have no choice. I'm either unwilling or unable to walk away from the temptress.

"We could both use a comfortable sleep. Tomorrow night will require a significant amount of energy on both our parts."

My blood heats to a near intolerable level with visions of how that energy will be spent. On the night of Dragobete, Luminita will learn the value of my touch. I'll make her crave it as much as I crave hers until she's as lost as I am in this sensual haze. Perhaps then she will understand the true meaning of submission.

13. An Old Wound

Luminita

The room above the tavern is not what I'd describe as spacious, but neither was my hut near the Timis River. Of course, I was never forced to *share* my small home. The place only has enough space for a bed pushed into one corner, a table with two chairs, a wooden chest, and a fireplace in the corner opposite the bed. Even those items are squeezed into the space.

As I stand on the threshold, staring in disappointment at the meager accommodations, Aaron steps up behind me. I can feel his warmth on my back, and it summons the feel of his body crushed against mine…the hard, impressive length of him trapped between us. The memory alone sends a decadent thrill through me, making my thighs clench.

Once again, I remind myself how dangerous he is…how easy it would be to lose control…how one lapse in judgment could cost me everything. I left my home in Kotor to maintain sole dominion over my fate. I will not relinquish any of it now.

Aaron almost touches me as he leans over my shoulder to peer into the cramped room. The smug satisfaction radiating from him only irritates me further.

"Rather tight quarters."

A heavy sigh rushes past my lips, and I step inside to place my pack on the bed while distancing myself from him. Then I dig some denarii from my pocket. Dragobete is always a profitable time, and in a city of this size, it is even more so.

When I turn around, he hovers far too close with the same raw desire I witnessed in the street earlier. With my jaw set and my glare sharp, I grab his hand and shove the coins into his palm. "Request a second room and get us something hot to eat."

The man bristles, but humor lingers in his signature. "Is that a command?" The low rumble of his voice vibrates through me, and I find it far too tempting.

My eyes narrow to slits. "Yes, Sălbatic."

Although his posture stiffens, the flash of anger is far weaker than I expected. Perhaps he somehow senses my arousal…his devious effect on me. That is a problem, which only hardens my resolve to approach the Dragobete rite the way I planned. It's a deviation, but a necessary one. I *must* maintain control.

When he doesn't move, I place a hand on his chest. His heart beats wildly against my palm. Only one heart, I note. Another deviation from the strigoi myths.

"Do *not* make me force the issue, Sălbatic. If you are not at peak strength, I will have no choice but to find a substitute for the rite, a human one if necessary."

This time his anger and a deep territorial urge flood my system like a torrent, and the glare in his silvery eyes is terrifyingly feral. "Luminita. If another man touches you, I will tear him limb from limb and drink him dry, regardless of the consequences." The primal words emerge as a clear threat. He means every single word, which both excites me, and rips open an old wound.

I use my palm to back him up a step. "I do *not* belong to you! I am not your *possession* to lord over like a ravenous dragon!" I push him back another step. "*You* do *not* decide *my* fate!" I shove him into the hall and slam the door before the shock fully registers on his face.

Draga & the Savage: Dragobete

A familiar rage sears through me until my hands shake. Fucking men and their need to claim territory. I am not some lifeless patch of dirt to be owned and worked.

Footsteps retreat down the hall and my pulse finally slows.

After unbinding my pack, I take the intricately carved gold bands and slip them beneath the straw mattress. They are far too precious to leave out in the open. The necklace, armlets, and belt are all I have left of the heirlooms my ancestors brought from Genoa.

Doubts begin to edge into my mind, and I undo my braid to run my fingers through the frazzled curls. I should look for a brush in the market tomorrow as well, or a comb at least. The calming motion helps me think as I pace the small space, but a brush would be best.

Aaron seemed to speak the truth earlier about the way wine and herbs affect him, but what if he omitted something? What if my concoction doesn't work? What if he doesn't succumb? What if I can't find the ingredients I require tomorrow? By the time I gathered enough coin, the vendors had retired for the evening.

Am I prepared to tread a dangerous line if my precautions are not an option? Perhaps involving the strigoi at all is too risky. Maybe I should simply find a strong male in town tomorrow for the rite. It would be far safer. I know how the herbs affect them.

But I've tried humans before with minimal results. If I want to rise above the societal limitations of my kind and my gender, risks must be taken. There is no great reward without it. If I wish to not only survive, but to rule and flourish, I must ensure the strigoi does not derail my plans.

I'm still pacing, running my fingers through my hair when a knock sounds at the door. I stop and stare at the plain wood, allowing my hands to drift back to my sides. "You may enter."

The door creaks open, and Aaron steps inside with two bowls. His stormy grey eyes only meet mine for a moment before shifting to the table. He says nothing as he maneuvers by me, sets the bowls down, and sinks into the far seat.

The intoxicating scent of stew makes my stomach growl and lures me to the table. Once I sit, he finally looks in my direction with obvious confliction.

"There are no other rooms," he states simply. "The city is flooded with villagers for Dragobete."

I nod thoughtfully, fearing that might be the case. After taking a bite of the savory stew, I peer around the room. "If we put the chairs on top of the table, there will be enough room for you on the floor."

Aaron pauses with his spoon halfway to his mouth and arches a brow. "The floor?" he asks incredulously.

"Yes." I return his stare with a firm one of my own.

He lets the spoon clatter into his bowl and straightens in his chair. "If *you* are not my possession, then *I* am not your dog, Luminita."

"You are not trustworthy in my bed." The words roll off my tongue before taking another bite, and the rage pulsing from the man is more intoxicating than any wine.

"At the river, I could have done anything to you while you slept. I did not touch you."

"You almost did," I say with a sly smile. "Or did you think I wouldn't know?"

The man swallows hard with an interesting myriad of emotions flickering through his signature before he sidesteps the question entirely. "I thought you wanted me at *peak strength,* or you'd *replace me.* Sleeping on a hard wooden floor is not likely to help matters."

I take another delicious bite and sink back into the chair, pondering the issue. My eyes dart to the trunk with an idea. After rising to my feet, I open the thing to find piles of linens and blankets. "There is enough to fashion you a bed of sorts," I say while peaking over my shoulder.

Aaron draws in a deep breath, his gaze hardening. "I am not sleeping on the floor."

I turn and straighten, planting my hands on my hips. "It seems were at an impasse."

"No, we are not," Aaron states in firm, clipped tones. "If you want me for your ritual, you will share the bed."

Draga & the Savage: Dragobete

The ultimatum amuses me, considering his earlier reaction to me finding a replacement. "And if I refuse? What will you do?"

An intriguing blend of emotions swirl through him but resolve emerges victorious. "I will leave."

My brow arches and I take a step forward. "Really?"

Although his jaw clenches and the now familiar heat between us intensifies, his mind is set. "Yes," he growls between gritted teeth.

Another step forward places me against his knee and the shiver of desire is beyond tempting. This is a dangerous game. Why even resist? I know he won't assault me in my sleep. He's right. The riverbank proved his restraint.

So, why toy with him over this? Because I can't help myself. The realization should be enough to make me stop, but it's not. Testing his granite resolve, flirting the treacherous line, seeing just how far I can push this magnificent specimen…it makes me feel alive in a way I've never felt.

I lean close until my breath mingles with his, my fingers almost touching his long dark hair. "And if I allow you to touch me this once, will you concede?"

Aaron's determination wavers, nearly lost in a bottomless ocean of erogenous hunger. Each panted breath washes over my lips, leaving them hot and moist. The urge to close the distance, to capture his mouth nearly claims me.

When he doesn't speak, my fingers drift into his hair and draw him so close our lips all but touch. The closeness of him…the tension writhing between us is the most potent aphrodisiac, and I find myself lost to it. I want to give in, to throw my carefully crafted plans to the wind, to experience something truly unique, to have one thrilling moment where I do not have to be in control.

"No," he whispers against my lips.

With one word, the moment shatters, and I pull back, unable to hide my shock. "What?"

Aaron's tongue darts across his lips while he draws in another deep breath, and his hands clench around his knees. "If touching you requires my humiliation…to sleep on the floor like a common animal…then I refuse your offer, even if it pains me to do so."

The rejection stings like a viper's bite and forces a derisive laugh from me. "You've already been on your knees for me twice, Sălbatic."

He casts a sharp glare and finally stands to tower over me, backing me up until my legs hit the trunk. "Not by choice."

Suddenly, I understand the distinction, and my anger quells. I meet his defiant stare and decide to concede this once. "Fine. We share the bed."

Suspicion lingers in his eyes as he continues to hover close. The intense pull snaps right back into place, and I struggle to maintain my composure.

"You will remain dressed, and you will *not* touch me." Even I can tell the resolve in my voice is weaker now.

One corner of his mouth tilts up slightly and he moves in, his lips almost touching mine again. "Is that what you really want, Draga?"

When he called me that in the street, it had been a mistake. I could sense his immediate regret and discomfort. However, this time, he speaks the word clear without hesitation. Draga…Romanian for beloved.

"Do not call me that," I whisper on a panted breath.

"Hmm. I rather like it." The gravelly tone travels straight through me, melting my core, and my brain screams an endless warning not to play with fire…to step away.

Once again, I place my palm on his chest and feel the furious, violent beat of his heart greeting my touch. "Don't," I whisper. "Please."

Something shifts behind his pale grey eyes, and he takes a step back.

Air rushes into my lungs and I can feel the flushed heat in my skin finally cooling.

"Do not toy with me, and I will not toy with you, Luminita," he states simply before kicking off his boots and climbing into bed. At least he takes the spot against the wall, so I don't have to climb over him. "Finish your stew and come to bed, Draga." The teasing tone grates every remaining nerve.

14. Draga

Aaron

My drowsy eyes open to sunlight streaming through the small window beside the fireplace. The harsh light cuts through the room directly toward the bed as if its sole purpose is to awaken sleeping guests. A groan escapes before I register the weight on my chest. I peer down to find a graceful hand resting on me. My gaze moves to the left and I find Luminita nestled against my shoulder. She looks almost docile when she sleeps, a stark contrast from her waking demeanor.

Although the morning sun burns my eyes, I don't move. I know as soon as I do, she'll recoil...pull away. Instead, I savor the rare moment of her unguarded yet unconscious affection. The woman is a lethal creature, but she surprised me last night. Perhaps her tell had not been intended, but I affected her just as deeply as she affected me. I saw it in her rapid breaths, her shaken resolve, the way her creamy skin blushed and heated, the dark of her eyes expanding until only a rim of blue remained.

Of course, recalling the way she looked at me last night immediately sends blood rushing to an inconvenient place. I close my eyes against the light and lean my head back into the pillow, trying to think of something besides those plump lips wrapped around my now throbbing erection.

I throw my free arm over my eyes with a stifled groan. How does this creature affect me so aggressively? The mere thought of her sends me into an undeniable sexual frenzy. Even in my youth...at the height of my carnal exploration, no one came close to causing this reaction, and it's been centuries since I desired to kiss a woman, much less anything else.

But last night...the compulsion to close the distance between us, to claim that wicked mouth, it almost undid me. I don't recall wanting anything more in my long life, not even blood. That I can attain rather easily, but *this* is a true challenge. Perhaps the reason I am so affected is because nothing has ever posed a threat to me. There is danger and risk here. If I push too far, Luminita can do more than simply put me on my knees.

A soft sound like a mewling little moan escapes her lips and every inch of me aches from it. For a moment, I find myself wondering if sinking into her tight heat would be worth incurring her possible wrath.

Luminita's cheek rubs against my linen shirt, drawing my attention back to the woman. Her eyes dart rapidly behind her lids, and I know the moment will be over soon. Dark eyelashes begin to flutter, and I quickly lay my head back down, closing my eyes.

Seconds later, her hand withdraws from my chest. I feel the mattress shift as she pulls away, and I mourn the loss of her touch. Then I hear her bare feet on the floor.

"We should eat before we venture into the market." Obviously, she knows I'm not sleeping.

I gaze over to see her sitting on the edge of the bed, facing the door.

When I don't answer, she looks over her shoulder at me. "Do you require time alone to deal with that first?" Her sea-blue eyes drift down to my crotch, and I swear the corner of her mouth lifts.

I clear my throat while reaching down to adjust myself, despite—or perhaps because of—her continued attention. "No. It will pass, unless..." I lean up on my elbow as her brow hikes. "...you'd like to lend your assistance."

Those voluptuous lips press into a line to keep from smiling, but she turns away and rises from the bed. The plain shift she wears hugs every curve, accentuating the hypnotic sway of her hips. "Conserve your strength, Sălbatic."

"I have plenty to spare, Draga."

Luminita's spine stiffens, and her hands pause over her pack. She glances over her shoulder again, but the stare is neither playful nor angry. It's something else I can't seem to place. "Do not call me that."

"Why?"

The woman's brow furrows. "Because it is an untrue name."

"No more than Dragaica," I counter, sitting up on the bed.

"To the people, I *am* the Lady of Flowers. It is not a false name."

"Then neither is Draga." My answer surprises me, but if anyone ever truly mattered to me in my seven thousand years of life, it is this strange and deadly goddess...this demoness of chaos I cannot walk away from.

I watch while Luminita paces back over to the bed, eyes studying me. She leans down, and my heart races. Then she slides her hands under the mattress on either side of me and she drags out the gold pieces she wore the first night I saw her.

Her gaze meets mine for a second, before she turns away again. "If you believe that, you are a fool," she says quietly.

I only stare at her in confliction while she slips on her black vest and pulls on her leather shoes. I'm not sure she means those words, but if she does...

I've never experienced heartache. It requires the ability to love... having a heart to break, but in this moment, I feel something akin to it.

"Put on your boots and meet me downstairs. I require your assistance procuring a few more items." She works her long hair into a loose braid to drape over her shoulder before heading for the door.

I say nothing and she doesn't wait for an answer.

When I finally venture downstairs, I find her sitting at a table, nibbling on cheese and a fresh loaf of bread. Her distant gaze is fixed on the front door where patrons are entering. She doesn't see me approach, but as I drag a chair out to sit, her attention snaps to me with a soft smile. The odd expression from earlier is gone.

"Eat," she says, gesturing at the food.

"What items do you need me to procure?" If she intends to pretend our little exchange this morning didn't happen, I won't press the issue. I upset her somehow, and to my surprise and annoyance, I care.

"Four torches, flint and iron, a stave of chestnut, a large mixing bowl, laurel for crowns, something to serve as a kantharos—the ritual cup—and lastly…" Her eyes lock onto mine and she leans in close to whisper. "A woman."

A deep frown pulls at my features. "A woman?"

Luminita peers around the room before whispering again. "Yes. For you. A blood sacrifice, although you may do whatever you want with her. It all lends to the Dionysian energy."

The very thought of touching a human in that way offends me. "For the blood sacrifice alone." I whisper back in a firm tone.

Her eyebrow arches while she leans back in her chair. "Suit yourself."

"It will just be the three of us then?" I try to keep the possessiveness out of my voice. It angered her last night, but the very thought of someone else touching her…having what I cannot…makes my blood boil.

Luminita considers me for a long moment, and I struggle to keep a grip on my territorial rage. "Yes," she finally concedes.

The relief is almost palpable. Had she intended to bring a man of her own, I would not be able to stop myself from rending him to tiny pieces. Although, in some Dionysian cults, the act would be welcomed as a violent expression of the divine frenzy.

"I'm curious," I say, sitting back in my chair. "Had we not crossed paths, how would you celebrate this festival? You seem to be lacking quite a few items. Ones you would not have found in Timisoara even before the Mongols."

Luminita takes another bite of bread while studying me. "I have a simpler rite I typically use. However, with a specimen such as yourself and a city market bursting with treasures, a more complex ritual should be used. Afterall, I want to take full advantage of you." An irrefutable heat lingers behind her words and once again…my body reacts. The woman's influence on me is problematic.

Draga & the Savage: Dragobete

After adjusting my *second* erection of the day and casting her a warning stare, she laughs. The woman laughs…a melodic and enchanting sound that plucks at my nerves.

"I'm glad I amuse you, *Draga.*" I emphasize the last word.

Her laughter fades and I almost regret saying it.

Luminita rises from her chair and takes a small hunk of cheese. "Eat and then find what you can. I'll meet you in the market later."

"Where are you going?"

The glare she throws at me this time is colder. "That is not your concern."

Irritation and anger bubble to the surface once more. "It is if you want my cooperation," I state in unconditional terms.

An aggravated sigh escapes her, and she stretches her neck. "Fine. There are a few herbs and resins I still need."

"See? Now was that so hard?" I smile smugly up at her until a mischievous glint lights those sea-blue eyes.

Luminita places her palms on the table and leans over it. Her lips nearly touch mine before she turns to whisper in my ear. "Not as hard as you are, Sălbatic."

Her teeth capture my earlobe, and she sucks it into her mouth, that devilish tongue flicking against it. My cock is immediately jealous and visions of that tongue moving against it instead dominate my thoughts.

As she pulls away, her gaze travels down to bear witness to the discomfort she's caused me.

"You should take care of that before you lock the room." The seductive tones only make things worse as she slides the key across the table.

"I thought I needed to conserve my strength," I counter.

A wicked grin curves her inviting mouth. "And I thought you had plenty to spare, Sălbatic."

15. Datura Seeds

Luminita

The large market is packed with people. A lot of them are travelers from smaller villages and towns who came to celebrate. It is rather common for Dragobete especially. Families bring their young men and maidens of marrying age to find a spouse. The unmarried men will venture out of the city and into the woods tomorrow morning in search of snowdrop or crocus flowers to present to their hopeful beloved.

The thought summons that infernal word. *Draga*. The man insists on using the name it seems, but he doesn't know its true meaning. How could he? Seven thousand years. I've not heard of a Durand living a tenth of that. When *everything* is fleeting in the world, how can you care about any of it?

Once again, warning bells chime in my head. Aaron is *not* human. Pulling energy from him had taken considerable effort. If things go wrong…if he discovers my plans… No. I have kept him sufficiently distracted. Of course, I know that is not the true reason I toy with him. Teetering on the edge with Aaron is too addictive.

After tonight, it won't matter. He'll most likely leave. I won't even blame him. I just hope I've instilled enough fear to keep him from ripping out my throat. That would negate all my hard work.

Jenny Allen

I head to the herb vendors first while Aaron is still preoccupied. After all, this is the most secretive part of my plan.

"Good morning, Dragaica," an older woman says as I approach her wares. "Thank you for blessing my goods with your presence on Dragobete of all days. Are you looking for something?"

"Yes. Salvia, of course. Laurel if you have it, *Mătrăguna*, and…" I hesitate with the final ingredient…the one that will either save or damn me. "Datura seeds."

The woman's eyes widen, stretching her wrinkles. "Datura seeds?"

"*Da*. They are for ritual use, not ingestion, of course."

"Of course." She forces a smile. "I do have some Datura…for healing pustules. There may be some seeds. I'll go look while you collect the other items you need. You should find them in one of the baskets." The woman emanates wariness as she disappears behind the curtain.

The laurel is easy enough to spot, and I collect enough to fashion three crowns. Whatever woman Aaron selects will need one. She may be no more than an offering, but even a sacrificial lamb must be presented to the gods with respect. The *Mătrăguna*, or Atropa Belladonna as the Greeks call it, takes longer to find. It is hidden in a small corner basket.

Salvia is commonly used during festivals, so a large basket brimming with the plant sits up front. I gather a handful of leaves, bypassing the purple flowers. They look pretty, but only the leaves hold the properties I require.

"You are in luck, Dragaica," The old woman says as she emerges from the curtain. "Is a dozen enough?"

I smile brightly. "It should be. Do you, by chance have a mortar and pestle you are willing to sell? The *Mătrăguna* and the Salvia must be ground." I do not mention the seeds. The only purpose in grinding them would be to poison someone.

"Yes, my lady." A deep frown wrinkles her face, and she hesitantly speaks. "I mean no offense, of course, but…it is rather heavy."

Her concern amuses me. "I am stronger than I look, I assure you."

Another hollow smile lifts her lips, and she packs my items into a basket for me.

Draga & the Savage: Dragobete

"I will take the Datura seeds. They are too dangerous to be misplaced."

She nods and hands me a little pouch, which I slip into my vest pocket before handing her more than enough Denarii.

"Dragaica, you are too generous." The woman tries to hand me a couple of coins back, but I refuse.

"For your service and your discretion."

She nods politely before gesturing to the basket.

Once I've ensured the *Mătrăguna* is buried beneath everything else, I haul the basket into my arms. For a human my size, it may have been a challenge, but the weight does not bother me. I stroll along the market, searching for resins. Although many use them for celebrations, they can be hard to come by at times. The Christian churches destroying the old traditions favor the resins for their services too.

While I'm browsing, someone takes the basket from my arms. I whirl around ready to fight off a thief only to find Aaron holding my purchases. I glare up at him and take the basket back.

"I am physically stronger than you," I whisper in clipped tones.

My irritation seems to amuse him. I suppose that is fair after my actions in the tavern. At least he found me *after* I completed my business with the herb vendor.

Aaron grins and begins to paw through the herbs. I yank the basket out of his reach with a scowl.

"Have you found any of the items I listed?"

"No," he replies with an odd smile. "I see you found the laurel on your own."

"I'm so happy to know you can identify simple plants." My aggravated tone only makes his smile widen. "Can you do something useful?"

With a smirk, he pulls out his empty pockets, and then leans closer. "You were so busy admiring my response to your tongue earlier, that you neglected to give me any coin for said items, Draga."

The vibration of his low voice elicits far too much of a response from me. Or perhaps it is his words and the memory of that rather delicious moment. I can feel the warm flush on my neck.

Jenny Allen

I shove the basket into his arms and carefully dig in my pockets, extracting a handful of Denarii. "Here. Now, go!"

Those silvery grey eyes study me as he holds the basket in one arm and accepts the coin. "What are you up to?" he asks while slipping the Denarii into his pocket.

"Nothing." Irritation and perhaps a twinge of fear ripple over my skin. At least he's not a Durand. He can't sense my apprehension.

Aaron merely stares at me, unconvinced.

"You do not have to be stitched to my side! Give me the key."

He complies with a curious expression.

"There is a lot to prepare, and it would be *helpful* if you procure the chestnut stave, torches, flint, a krater, and something to act as a kantharos. I'll be in the room later." I snatch the basket from his arm and storm off toward the next vendor. Much to my relief, Aaron does not follow.

Once I've found a few resins, including frankincense, I make my way back to the inn. The tavern is packed now. The crowd is boisterous, but not rowdy. The wine and mead are not yet flowing this early in the afternoon.

Still, pushing past the mostly male patrons with my heavy basket proves challenging. Several times I'm knocked off balance to teeter into others, and more than once I feels hands in undesirable places. No one seems to take offense but me.

The overwhelming weight of so many vigorous celebrations already has me on edge, and the constant press of bodies jostling me only darkens my mood. The men who grope me as I pass are lucky to keep their lecherous hands. By the time I reach the back stairs, the desire to drain the lot of them gnaws at my insides. Power in numbers, I remind myself. Creating a scene here…with so many…would not end well for me.

Pain cuts through my mind like a finely sharpened axe as I trudge up the stairs. Headaches are not common, but when assaulted by so many potent emotions, it is almost a guarantee, which is why I typically avoid larger cities. Only rest and quiet—away from others—will ease the pain, but I have work to do first.

Draga & the Savage: Dragobete

After unlocking the door, I enter the thankfully vacant room and drop the basket on the table. My gaze trails to the bed when another stab of pain strikes. I rub my temples and sigh longingly. I want nothing more than to sleep away this torment, but I cannot afford to waste this time alone. Aaron could return unexpectedly, and locking the door will only delay him for so long.

My heart feels heavy when I insert the key to lock the room. It must be the headache and aftereffects from downstairs. But…the sensation doesn't lessen as it should now that I'm alone. It only seems to grow more acute when I pull out the cast iron mortar and pestle.

After tossing the Belladonna into the mortar, I pull the small bag from my vest and tip the Datura seeds into my palm. I stare down at them with heaviness and indecision nearly suffocating me. Perhaps it isn't the crowd downstairs causing my discomfort at all. Maybe it is the dangerous seeds in my hand which resemble tiny river stones. Maybe it is the line I'm about to cross.

The moment in the market returns to me—the way Aaron's deep dimpled lines bracketed his sly smile…his low, raspy tone when he called me Draga again…the teasing spark between us…the way I feel drawn to him as if he were the moon itself.

What if we can be true partners? Equals? What if I do not need to submit in order to have him…enjoy him?

Fantasies, I realize. His reaction last night said as much. When I threatened to replace him, he responded with feral dominance. He'll kill any man who touches me…as if I am a priceless trinket to be coveted and locked away. Aaron is thousands of years old and has never conceded to anyone.

The man has said please and obeyed my requests, but *only* because I displayed my ability to harm him. If given a choice…given free will, he would exert his perceived dominion over me. He will never consider me an equal.

An eerie sadness fills me, and I toss the Datura seeds into the mortar. I have no choice. This is the only way to ensure I remain in control tonight…the only way to be truly safe.

Jenny Allen

I grind the Belladonna and Datura before adding some of the Salvia, but not all. I set aside a few leaves of the lightly hypnotic plant for myself. Wine and Salvia are required for the rite. Once I work the concoction into a fine powder, I pour the blend into the small bag.

Despite being alone and the relaxation of grinding the herbs, my head still throbs painfully. Now that the contraband is unrecognizable, I can finally rest. After tucking the pouch into my pack, I curl up on the straw mattress and pull the blanket over me to block out the light.

16. Blood in Crystal Form

Aaron

My mind wanders while I stroll around the busy market. I find it difficult to focus on my given tasks. Luminita was…troubled when I saw her out here. Her irritation was different than the versions I've seen. Not playful or wrathful…more nervous. Perhaps she feels some pressure to complete this rite of hers the proper way.

I don't believe in it. I don't see how wine, herbs, blood, and sex will grant her any special power. In fact, if she intends to consume any of *my* blood, it might very well kill her. No human has survived its consumption. Duncan proved its lethality many times during his research. Although she hasn't mentioned my blood being an element, I should probably warn her.

An all too familiar irritation makes my skin itch. Two days ago, I cared about no one's life but my own. Then *she* appeared, like a Goddess of blood and chaos.

With a heavy sigh, I focus my attention on the various booths. I find the chestnut stave first. Unsurprising, since it's quite commonly used in a variety of traditions, including Dragobete. I stroll past several more vendors before I find the krater. The large clay mixing bowl should suffice. The torches, flint and steel are common enough and easy to find.

Jenny Allen

The kantharos however, eludes me. There are plenty of cups and even a few simple chalices, but not something worthy of Luminita's rite.

I may have no faith in her plan, but she does, and I feel compelled to help Luminita achieve her vision. Part of me wonders if it's just the allure of finally conquering her that motivates me. I can still feel her soft hair between my fingers from the first time I touched her, the weight of her hand on my chest, and the warmth of her mouth wrapped around my earlobe. The tension between us is beyond intoxicating and I know, without a doubt, the moment we *truly* collide will shake the world.

The very thought makes me hard, which is far from convenient in a busy marketplace. I carry the krater low to conceal what I can, but everyone seems intent on their own transactions, much to my relief.

I continue to browse, searching for the one perfect item, and I know it's not just sex compelling me to do so. The carnal acts have never been of importance to me. The challenge is what matters. In all my years, she is the first to do so. Luminita is not some fair maidan who faints at the sight of blood, blindly follows orders, or cowers to *any* man, human or not. She is shrewd, fearless, vicious, powerful, and commanding. A rare beauty complete with thorns among a world of weeds. A pinpoint of light in an ocean of darkness.

Like the creation myth of *Fîrtat*, Luminita shines in her truth. She does not hide or pretend she is anything else. Not even my brothers can claim that. She is more my equal than they ever were.

I pause on the thought…equal. It's not a notion I've ever considered, but then no one else has put on my knees or made me ask permission for *anything*. It's an odd feeling…experiencing something new after thousands of years. I thought the world held no more mysteries for me to solve. I thought I'd seen and experienced everything of importance.

"Pardon, sir," a man says as he bumps my shoulder and quickly rushes past me.

I expel an aggravated sigh and force my mental rambling into the background. I still have a mission to complete before I can return to our little room.

After an exhaustive search, I manage to locate a booth with a few antiquities. The silver chalice I find there is far more elaborate than the others I've seen. The delicate carvings of trees are quite lovely and the small green gems around its base glint in the sun.

As I hand the vendor the chalice to wrap, my eyes drift to a stone dangling from a long gold chain. The ruby is small, but tear shaped like a drop of blood. How very fitting.

"This as well," I say, handing him the necklace.

"Very good, sir." The man wraps it in a small piece of red cloth.

I pass him the rest of my coin, one or two more than requested, and place the wrapped items in the krater before maneuvering through the growing crowd. There are far too many humans in this city.

It's rather late in the afternoon by the time I climb the tavern stairs toward our room. I balance my items in one arm while grabbing the door, but find it locked. My knock is greeted with silence. Perhaps she hasn't returned. I don't recall seeing her among the people downstairs.

I knock once more, louder this time, and finally hear soft footsteps approach. The lock clicks and the door swings open to reveal Luminita's back as she walks to the bed and sits on the edge.

My brows immediately draw together in concern. "What's wrong?"

She peers up at me for a moment, before rubbing her temple. "When I got back, I had a difficult time getting upstairs." Luminita straightens, stretching her neck. "It made my head ache and I had to lie down. I'm fine." A half-hearted smile stretches her full lips.

I slide the krater laden with goods onto the table beside her basket and mortar, then prop the stave against the chair. "What do you mean by a *difficult time*?"

A soft sigh escapes her while she undoes her braid and runs her fingers through her hair in an almost idle motion, as if it soothes her. "It was crowded, and I don't exactly *look* imposing. It doesn't matter. That many people emanating powerful emotion takes its toll. Did you find what we need?"

"Yes, actually. Everything on your list."

The tired persona evaporates and a wicked grin graces those tempting lips. "Not everything, apparently." She peers back at the door as if expecting someone before capturing my gaze again. "I do not see a woman."

For some unknown reason, this irritates me. "Why must this offering be a woman?"

Luminita's eyebrows lift in surprise. "Does it make a difference to you? Man, woman, child, whatever your preference."

My eyes narrow. "To drink."

The woman laughs in amusement. "Yes, Sălbatic. To drink only."

"This rite of yours. Does it require my blood?"

The laughter stops and her head tilts, considering me while she continues to comb her fingers through her hair. The motion is hypnotic and the urge to touch it is nearly irresistible. "Some," she finally admits.

"You can't ingest it," I state firmly.

"Why?" Curiosity sparks those maddening blue eyes.

"It's lethal."

"To humans," she adds.

"Yes, but I don't know what it would do to you."

She shrugs and rises from the bed, pacing toward me. "I appreciate your concern, Sălbatic, but I won't be drinking it." She stops with only inches between us, her eyes capturing mine, as if searching for something.

The ache to pull her against me is difficult to resist, especially when I can see her pebbled nipples straining against the thin shift.

She leans past me, her chest grazing my arm as she reaches for the packages in the krater. "Let's see what you've found."

When she straightens, I grab the item wrapped in red cloth, and she peers up at me with sudden interest.

"What is that?"

"Open the other first," I say, fighting a smile.

Her sea-blue eyes narrow, but a grin plays across her plump lips. "Secrets?"

I merely lift my chin toward the package in her hands.

Luminita smirks. "Fine." She delicately unfolds the fabric to reveal the silver chalice and her face lights. "It's beautiful." Delicate fingers trace along the carved trees and green gems with a look of wonder.

"Close your eyes."

Draga & the Savage: Dragobete

She raises a stern brow and glares up at me. "Why?"

A chuckle rumbles in my chest and I can't honestly recall the last time I've laughed in good humor. "Not everything is a challenge for dominance, Draga. Please."

Her glare doesn't soften, but with an irritated sigh, she does as I asked.

I take a second to appreciate the dark lashes resting against her pale skin, the slight curve of her full lips, the way her raven-black hair frames her face. A seemingly delicate beauty hiding such ferocity, and in this moment, she shows me trust, even if it is begrudgingly so.

After I pull the necklace from its wrapping, I let the red fabric flutter to the ground. Gently gripping the long chain, I slip it over her head. I'm not ashamed to admit I savor the feel of her soft tresses against my skin while I lower the necklace. Once in place, my fingers trail over the chain until they touch the tear-shaped stone resting between her breasts just shy of the shift's neckline. A slight blush greets my touch and I swallow hard before forcing myself to take a step back.

I finally drag my gaze back to her face. She wears a slight frown and slowly opens her eyes. Intrigue and perhaps...pain burn in their oceanic depths while she holds my stare.

"A present for your rite," I say somewhat stiffly and nod toward the pendant. The moment feels uncomfortable for some reason. Although don't all things feel that way the first time? I've never given a gift. The act implies things I've not experienced in my time upon this earth. Maybe I didn't present it properly.

Luminita's fingertips glide along the chain as mine did before she looks down at the pendant...a drop of blood in crystal form resting against her pale skin. Her brow furrows as she stares at it and my discomfort grows. Perhaps I was too impetuous...too caught up in our little dance.

After what seems like an eternity—an irony not lost on me considering my age—Luminita's face tilts up to mine. The hurt and almost ambivalent expression is *not* what I expected.

"Is this an attempt to buy my affections? Is it so easy to put a price on me?"

I frown with fresh irritation, but it doesn't boil over into rage as it would have a day ago. The woman makes nothing easy, but then...is that not why I find her so fascinating? "Considering I used your coin to purchase it, no."

The skin around her eyes tightens and she pins me in place with her questioning stare, obviously unsatisfied with my answer. "Why did you buy this?"

Defensive anger is my initial reaction, but again, it doesn't last. Luminita has not lived as long as I have, but longer than most...long enough to not trust easily, to see danger where there may not be any, and we are still strangers. The compulsion to ease *her* discomfort overrides my concern for my own. Yet another first.

Slowly, I unclench my jaw and take a step closer. I choose boldness. When my hands slip along her neck, she flinches, but doesn't pull away. She merely stares at me as I sweep her hair up, freeing it from the chain. I allow it to fall against her shoulders once more and remove my hands from her. Every fiber of my being wants to grip her nape and pull her to me...to taste those tempting lips, but I step back again.

"It seemed fitting for a Goddess of blood and chaos."

The animosity leaks from her expression, and her gaze falls to the floor in what I can only describe as sadness. The woman never reacts the way I predict she will.

"If you don't like it—"

"No," she says softly. "I do. It's just..." Luminita hesitates and her gaze lifts to mine again. "...unexpected."

An amused grin cracks my worried expression. "From my observations, humans usually find surprises pleasurable."

Luminita's dark brows draw together. "I am not human, Sălbatic, and neither are you."

My grin broadens and a lustful hunger leaks into my voice. "I am very well aware of that fact, Draga."

Her fingers caress the small stone as we stare at each other, the now familiar heat building between us, drawing me to her. I move to close the distance that feels almost painful, but she blinks and turns toward the table.

Draga & the Savage: Dragobete

"I should weave the laurel crowns. It's getting late." The words sound forced, but I grant her the reprieve she obviously requires. Tonight, during her ritual, she won't turn from me. Dionysus is all about embracing the frenzy...indulgence. Seven thousand years has taught me some measure of patience.

"Where will we perform this ceremony of yours?" I move past her to the bed and sit, giving her space to work.

"One of the villagers spoke of a secluded mineral spring at the foot of Deva hill."

"I know the spot."

She turns to peer at me inquisitively, but my gaze fixes on the red stone glinting against her creamy flesh. The contrast is quite arousing. "You've been here to Deva before?"

"Yes, although it was called Decidava back then. Many, many years ago, when it was little more than a farming town."

She nods in thought and slips into the chair facing me. Her gaze falls to the pendant before she meets my eyes again. "Is this surprise of yours why you did not return with a blood offering?"

"No."

The answer seems to relieve her, though I'm unsure why. She grabs a strand of laurel and begins working it. "Why then?"

I find the question rather annoying. I expected her to know the answer by now. Perhaps she does but wishes me to confirm it. "I prefer not to spend my time in the company of humans. They only serve *one* purpose to me."

This seems to pique her interest. She glances up at me while she continues to weave the vine. "So, you do not *play* with your food?" The seductive way she emphasizes the one word makes her meaning quite clear.

A huffed laugh escapes and I lean forward, bracing my arms on my knees. "Not in an *extremely* long time."

Luminita smiles broadly at me, her fingers absently working the laurel. "When was the last time you had sex?"

Jenny Allen

The boldness of this woman should no longer shock me, but it does. "Too long to recall."

Her eyebrows lift and her fingers pause. "Ten years? One hundred?"

"Thousands."

Luminita stares at me incredulously.

"Humans lost their appeal to me before I left Sumer."

Her gaze drops to the laurel in her hands, and she resumes weaving. "I must admit, that is not the response I expected considering your…" Ocean-blue eyes meet mine with the devilish heat I crave so intently. "…frequent and enthusiastic reactions to me."

A wicked grin slowly creeps over my lips. "As we have established, Draga, you are *no mere human*."

"True." Luminita's grin widens, and I spot a faint blush coloring her cheeks. Her teeth rake over her bottom lip, and she peeks up at me again in mischievous delight. "After so much time, are you sure you remember how?"

I drop the façade, letting her see every bit of my burning desire and lean back on the bed, propped up on my elbows. "I'm perfectly willing to prove my worth, Draga."

Luminita lets out an amused sound resembling a soft moan and her gaze rakes down my body to the hard evidence of my arousal. "Should I be flattered by your response to me then?" she asks, bypassing my offer. Ever the evasive tactician it seems.

I eye her for a moment, trying to decide how much of my jugular to expose to her. But…I've never been a creature of subtlety. Why start now? "Luminita. You are the first person my cock has wanted in thousands of years, the first person to ever force me to pleasure myself out of sheer desperation, the first person I've ever felt compelled to give a gift. Should you be flattered that an uncaring monster feels less so in your presence? Perhaps not."

Once again, her hands pause in midmotion, and she stares at me with the same sadness she showed after I gifted her the necklace. "I do not consider you a monster." She places the laurel crown on top of the basket and leans forward, the red pendant swaying. "You are a vicious god among men. You should be feared yes, but also revered, and tonight you shall be my Dionysus."

I don't recall any words spoken to me having carried such significance, and it takes every ounce of my strength to remain seated on the bed.

17. Draga meu

Luminita

Aaron lies on the bed with his arms folded behind his head, contently watching me as I weave the laurel crowns. His gaze feels like a burning touch. I cannot deny the way he melts my core with his words alone at times, much less his heated touch. I still feel his fingers on my neck, soft and sensual. Is it possible for a touch to leave a permanent impression? Perhaps it is the emotion behind it lingering on my skin.

The thought brings back the heaviness in my heart, and once again I question the Datura seeds' necessity. Even his moments of anger quickly withered beneath other…stronger emotions. Perhaps he intends me no harm. Maybe he is earnest in his pursuit.

The light glints off the ruby pendant, capturing my attention for a moment. It looks like a drop of blood against my skin. Blood. The one thing sacred to him. It doesn't matter that he used my coin to purchase it. There is *meaning* behind it, and perhaps that scares me more than his anger.

I peek up to see him still watching me, a slight smile on his lips. "Do you know how to weave?"

The smile broadens. "I do not."

"Because it's a woman's work?" My voice sounds bitter, but I fight the urge to return his smile.

"Because I've had no need to learn," he responds simply. "I take what I want in this life." A wicked smile plays across his inviting mouth. "With one notable exception, that is."

A laugh breaks through as I finish the first crown and put it aside to start the next. "Is that why you are so…enamored with me?"

"In part," he admits. "You are the first in many ways, Draga."

His rather bold confessions unnerve me. It would be so easy to simply give in, but that means sacrificing the only thing I've valued in my life— control. Human or not, this world does not value women. The Durand taught me how little I mattered. We are not on equal footing with men. Love in this world means sacrificing yourself, giving yourself over to another, obedience, devotion, servitude. I refuse to comply with those societal demands for anyone…even Aaron.

"Tell me more about the steps in your ritual."

I lift my eyes back to him while I weave. "We will require an open space with one torch at each of the four points. You shall stand in the center with your blood sacrifice while I cast the circle. Then I'll prepare the resins and herbs for burning, and the ceremonial wine. After I've anointed you both and you anoint me, you will drink from your offering. Then you'll drink from the chalice, and we shall let the frenzy consume us." The last part passes my lips with a decadent grin.

Regardless of how things play out and the precautions I take, I will have him, and the thought makes my thighs clench tight. The teasing dance we've perfected will result in a collision of souls.

"And the part which requires my blood?"

I've expected the question and am rather surprised he didn't ask earlier. Still, it fills me with apprehension. If I answer truthfully, there is a chance he will refuse, but… I glance over at my pack and feel the weight of the lies it contains.

"The rite requires I mark you as the god Dionysus."

"Mark me?" The words carry a note of suspicion but also amusement.

"A small sigil on your chest." I meet his questioning gaze once more. "I do not intend to hurt you, Sălbatic." *Not physically at least.* The intrusive thought sours my stomach, and I shift in my seat, refocusing on my work.

Draga & the Savage: Dragobete

Aaron remains silent, watching me finish the second and third crowns. I try to ignore his gaze and take his silence as consent.

Once they are done, I tuck the mortar and pestle under the table. I have no further need of them. Then I gather everything into the krater and the basket from the herb vendor, including the two bottles of wine.

"I need you to leave the room," I state firmly while pulling my gold adornments and crimson dress from my pack.

When he doesn't respond, I peer over my shoulder to witness a wide grin on his face.

"Why?"

"Because I would like to change in peace," I answer with irritation.

"I saw everything by the river, Draga. *You* ensured that."

Although his lustful gaze is quite arousing, I need a moment away from the shifting emotions emanating from him…a moment of quiet to solidify my convictions…to not feel this odd guilt weighing on my heart.

"That does not mean I owe you a show. Out!" I snap wearily.

The man rises from the bed with a knowing smile. My orders used to anger him, but now…they seem to amuse him even if he does obey. I find it aggravating and insulting, as if he is merely humoring a child.

While I glower at him indignantly, he steps close, leaving only inches between us. The pull…the thrum of energy…is immediate whenever he stands this close. I can feel his body heat caressing my skin, and I ache for his touch. He stares down at me with those silvery eyes, his long dark hair spilling over his shoulders to frame his face. My breath hitches and the compulsion to taste his lips nearly irradicates my other thoughts.

"As you wish, Draga. I can be a patient man." His lips hover over mine, but never touch. The exhilaration surging through my body steals my breath for a moment, and I latch onto his arm when my knees almost buckle. "Unless you've changed your mind."

He slides an arm around my waist to steady me, growing bold, and although the action makes my heart beat violently against my ribs, I push him away. "I have not." I say in a colder tone than I intend.

Aaron studies me for a moment before dipping his head. "I will wait for you downstairs, but I have one request."

I release a frustrated sigh. "What is it?"

He gathers up the krater and basket packed with items, moving silently for the door. I hurry to open it for him, and he pauses on the threshold. When he looks back at me, his eyes are filled with violence. "Wrap a blanket around yourself before you leave this room wearing *that* dress. There are too many humans in this city, and if a man dares to touch you, I will tear out his throat."

My anger swells just as it had the first time he made such a statement, but before I can speak, he continues.

"*Not* because you are my property, but because you are not *his*."

He slips into the hall while I'm still weighing his words.

Before I leave the room, I wrap the blanket around myself and grab the chestnut stave leaning against the table. Aaron is right. The dress is rather provocative with its sheer crimson fabric held in place only by the gold band at my throat and the gold belt. I experienced enough groping hands earlier when wearing normal clothes.

When I step into the packed tavern, the crowd is rowdier than before, and I focus all my energy into blocking out the stifling press of emotions. I start to push my way through the crowd, but a few steps in, an arm grabs me and tugs me against them. I turn, expecting to see Aaron, only to be greeted by the leering grin of a stranger. I move to shove him away, but another man crashes into my back, pinning me to the first one's chest.

Before I can even pull at the intoxicated stranger's essence, a hand grips his throat and a deep voice full of lethality rumbles through the air. "Unhand her or I will tear out your damn throat."

As the human throws up his hands, my eyes travel up to Aaron's face hovering above the stranger's shoulder. The wrathful violence I'd witnessed in his eyes that first night blazes in them now. Aaron pulls the man back a step and whispers in his ear with a vicious sneer, but I can't hear what he says over the noisy crowd. Then he tosses the man to the floor and his gaze shifts to me. The terrifying expression melts with each passing second as he stalks up to me and bends to whisper against my ear.

Draga & the Savage: Dragobete

"Grant me permission to touch you so I can get you out of here. Please, Draga. If another man grabs you, I won't be able to control myself."

I don't need his help. I could have weakened both men and shoved them away. I can force my way through the crowd, but if he loses control in a city like this, it could damn us both. Beyond that…I want to accept his offer…to feel no one else's hands on me…only his.

I nod just as someone bumps into me from behind, shoving me against Aaron. In one quick movement, he sweeps me up into his arms, and storms through the crowd. Once we reach the open sky I can finally breath and Aaron's chest rises and falls rapidly against me. Suddenly, I am very aware of every place our bodies touch, and my gaze drags up to his stormy grey eyes. Their depths are overwhelming and for a moment, I forget about all of it—the crowd, the city, Dragobete, the ritual, control, everything.

Aaron's throat bobs and I feel the maddening desire as if it's my own. Perhaps it is. The pack I carry seems heavier now and I know it's the Datura seeds plaguing my mind again.

"Sir." A young woman's voice intrudes on the moment, but when her hand touches Aaron's arm, the moment shatters completely. Some foreign feeling like anger gnaws at my stomach.

"Put me down, Sălbatic."

His gaze never leaves mine, completely ignoring the girl, but he complies. Once he gently places me on my feet, his ambivalent stare turns to the intrusive woman.

"I've got your things here," she says meekly before she turns her attention to me. "Lady of Flowers." The maid utters my name with reverence. "I'm honored to be of assistance to you. Your consort said you wanted me to assist you with a special rite for Dragobete."

I cast Aaron a sideways glance. "Consort?"

A smug smile tugs at his lips. "Is that not what I am, Dragaica?"

"Of course, Sălbatic. *Tonight* you are my consort." My emphasis on *tonight* makes him prickle, but I turn away to face the young maiden, truly taking her in for the first time.

Jenny Allen

She's pretty in a humble sort of way with flowers woven into her light brown hair. Color fills her tanned cheeks, and her hazel eyes shine with wonder. The maiden's slender frame is swallowed by her traditional clothing, an embroidered white blouse and a skirt of thick red and black fabric.

"Yes," I say with a sweet smile. "We require your help."

I adjust my pack, grip the stave, and weave an arm through hers. "Show us to the mineral springs, sweet one."

The girl beams at me. "Of course, Lady of Flowers."

I glance over my shoulder and grin at Aaron's irritated expression while he gathers the krater and basket, hauling them into his arms. When he catches me watching, his signature changes. Irritation is replaced by longing, and I become acutely aware of the pendant lying over my heart.

Once we arrive at the secluded clearing tucked against the hill, I lead the woman to its center. "Remain here, while I prepare."

She nods eagerly.

"Sălbatic, you can place those here." I indicate a spot a few feet away from our guest.

He does as directed without complaint. "How can I help?"

"I shall place the torches at the four points, if you can light them for us?"

A slow spreading smile creeps across his lips, but he says nothing.

When I place the first torch, he approaches with the flint and steel, still wearing that secretive smile.

"What is so amusing?" I whisper.

"Not amusing."

"Then what are you smiling about?" I ask, irritation edging into my voice.

Aaron leans closer to whisper, his lips brushing my ear, which sends a delicious shiver down my spine. "The thought of your naked body by torch light and *all* the ways I want to drive your frenzy and bring you to divine bliss. I've never wanted something more, Draga."

The words alone make me slick with desire, but fear also accompanies them. The fear of losing control...of being lost to him. Dionysus is a god-like representation of exactly that, and yet I seek to prevent it for myself. Perhaps that makes me a hypocrite, but survival will drive a woman to desperate measures.

In another bold move, he unwraps the blanket from around me and tosses it aside.

"Out here, you don't need to hide." The backs of his fingers coast down my shoulder in a faint caress. "Out here, you are the Goddess of Blood and Chaos." His touch lingers on the tear-shaped ruby before those enigmatic eyes capture mine again. "*Draga meu.*"

My beloved.

18. Collision of Souls

Aaron

The Ancient Greeks believed a person had two souls—a mortal one responsible for life and consciousness, and an immortal one responsible for emotions, dreams, and the afterlife. I have never believed in the second type, the one Luminita claims to consume.

However, as I stand in the center of the torchlit clearing, staring into the bewitching eyes of this goddess, I wonder. Perhaps only those above humanity have a soul. What if the concept eluded me for thousands of years? What if it took another divine creature to draw mine into the light? *This* enthralling creature, in particular.

Plato once spoke about souls cleaved in half by jealous gods and sent to wander the earth in search of their other half. I thought him a sentimental fool at the time, but what if the human was right? What if *that* is the true reason I am so drawn to my Goddess of blood and chaos?

Luminita holds my stare as she rests the laurel crown on my head, and I feel lost to her...moved to believe in things I never thought possible. She rises on tiptoe to press a kiss to my cheek. Her lips linger and warm breath washes over my skin, deepening my already maddening hunger for her. My body tenses to resist pulling her against me, and when she steps back, the loss of her heat leaves a hollow pit in my stomach.

Luminita holds out the second laurel crown to me. I accept it, letting my greedy fingers drift over her hands with a compulsive need to touch her...an ache that already seems heightened in this sacred place.

I settle the ring of leaves upon her raven-black tresses and allow myself another indulgence. My fingers slips through her hair, savoring the silky strands. I bow to press my lips to her blushing cheek and stay there. I don't want to pull away and leave the moment. I want to stay right here in her warmth, but that is not the will of my goddess.

Luminita steps back, but when her eyes meet mine, the hesitation in them gives me hope. Perhaps she craves me as much as I crave her. Maybe she longs for my touch too.

Reluctantly, her eyes shift to the maidan beside me. Although Luminita gently places the final crown on the human's head, she leaves only a brief kiss on the girl's cheek before turning away.

Flickering light shimmers over the iridescent fabric as Luminita takes the stave and saunters toward the perimeter. When she stops in front of the first torch, the dress glows like divine fire, revealing her seductive silhouette in a dazzling display. Then she thrusts the stave skyward and throws her head back, and the air seizes in my lungs. If anyone could make me believe in magic and souls, it's *Draga meu*.

"I call upon loud-roaring and reveling Dionysus." She chants the words with firm command while she paces the circle, and I track every movement with wonder and unquenchable desire.

"Primeval, double-natured, thrice-born." Luminita passes the second torch and once again, the light reveals her sinful body. "Bacchic lord, wild, ineffable." She passes the third torch, and it bathes her skin in warmth. "Secretive, two-horned and two-shaped." She saunters past the fourth torch and continues to complete the circle. "Ivy-covered, bull-faced, warlike, howling pure."

The mystical goddess stops where she began and holds the stave higher. "We call upon thee!" Her voice booms through the night, and the girl beside me shrinks, reminding me of her presence.

After a moment, Luminita lowers the chestnut stave, turns, and proceeds toward the supplies gathered near the circle's center.

Draga & the Savage: Dragobete

"Do you require assistance, Dragaica?" the maid asks, stepping forward, but I snatch the intrusive girl's arm.

Luminita casts a ruthless glare over her shoulder. "No," she growls. "Remain silent."

Much to my annoyance, the thing continues to speak. "But I don't understand my part, Lady of Flowers."

Anger surges to the surface, and I tug at her arm, but Luminita holds up a hand. I watch in rapt attention as the deadly glare of my goddess morphs into a sweet smile.

"You will soon, child." Luminita's gaze snaps to mine and I can almost feel the excitement in their depths. "Soon." The intimate way the word rolls off her tongue sharpens my anticipation.

Luminita turns back to her work, organizing components. She tosses herbs and resins into the clay bowl. The flint strikes steel, lighting her face with stunning flashes of light, only enhancing her divine visage.

Soon, echoes in my mind, but it's not the blood I ravenously crave. Every stitch of my body screams for the goddess before me, as if nothing else exists. Some distant part of me wonders if she's somehow bewitched me, cast a spell to keep me enthralled, but if so...I don't care.

Luminita reaches into her pack and pulls out a small pouch. For the first time since our arrival here, she seems to hesitate. She stares at the small bag, but I can't see much of her face from this angle. I'm curious about what might give her pause, but the moment passes. After dumping the powdery substance into the chalice, she fills it with wine. Then she draws a thin dagger from her pack and uses it to stir the concoction.

Aromatic smoke from the krater swirls around her enticing form. A gentle breeze rustles the sheer dress and her dark tresses. The silver chalice rests in her hands, and as she approaches, I realize something. In *this* moment, Draga would not need to *force* me to my knees. I would fall to them willingly...for *her*.

Luminita's eyes remain fixed on the chalice while stepping before the maidan. The slender human appears to be scared, as she should be. She stands between two gods, separating them...an obstacle I am all too eager to remove. But all things in time.

Draga dips her finger into the wine and traces three circles in a pyramid formation on the girl's forehead. "The sigil of grapes…an offering." Tremors course through the little human, tickling against my hand still locked around her arm, but she says nothing.

When Luminita's intense gaze slides up to mine with carnal heat, it sets my fledging soul aflame. I summon all my strength to simply stand still when she steps in front of me. Once again, she dips her finger in the wine.

I bow slightly, allowing her to reach my forehead easier, but my eyes never leave hers.

"The sigil of the cup," she speaks softly while her finger traces a pattern upon my skin. "It symbolizes the receptacle for the offering." I start to stand straight, but she leans closer to whisper in sultry tones. "Remove your clothes, Sălbatic." Those words set more than my soul on fire.

While Luminita paces backward, hips swaying, her heated stare rakes over me from my bare feet up to my linen shirt. Instead of pulling the fabric over my head and risk marring the sigil she's traced, I rip the shirt and let the tatters fall to the ground.

The sight of Luminita's teeth sinking into her bottom lip almost undoes me. My already hard cock twitches before my freehand unbuckles my belt. The loose pants fall to the ground and the human gasps, but her reaction is not the one I seek.

Even in the firelight, I see the dark of Luminita's eyes engulf the blue and her breaths quicken. The anticipation of the moment we collide is torturous, twisting and pulling me in one inevitable direction…the *only* direction…toward my beloved.

"When the sigil of the cup and the grapes combine, Dionysus is reborn." Luminita places the chalice on the ground and steps away from it, but movement distracts us both. The young woman wrestles her arm away from my distracted grip and runs, tears streaming down her face.

I catch her in a few quick strides, clamping an arm around her waist, and drag her back.

"No! Please!" The thing cries and squirms until I firmly plant her back to my chest and squeeze her throat.

"Silence," I warn in a low growl. "Behave or I'll make things painful, human."

"Please, Sir! I've never laid with a man. Please!"

The very thought nearly turns my stomach. "I have no interest in your body, girl," I snarl in disgust. "Be still!"

The sniveling thing finally stops fighting, and I peer up to see Luminita drinking deeply from the second bottle of wine. The sensual way her head is tilted back immediately brings the moment back to me.

My goddess drops the bottle. Her voracious eyes fix on me as her tongue darts across her lips, savoring the sweetness. "Take your offering and be reborn." The reverent command stirs everything inside me, not only because I can quiet this little beast in my arms, but also because it brings me one step closer to the only woman I covet.

My intense stare doesn't waver from my Goddess of blood and chaos while I pull the girl's head to the side, or when my fangs unfold.

Luminita watches me intently, her chest heaving beneath the shimmering fabric. The maidan screams when the sharp points graze her skin, but the sound barely registers. It's insignificant like most things…everything but the enchanting creature before me.

Draga doesn't shy away or avert her gaze. No. The woman's hunger magnifies when my teeth pierce the girl's skin. A rivulet of crimson spills down the shrieking human's chest, staining her white blouse, and I drink.

"You take raw flesh, you have feasts, wrapped in foliage, decked with grape clusters, resourceful, Ebouleus, *Immortal god* sired by Zeus. When mated with Persephone in unspeakable union."

Every word she chants sears into my skin like a brand, heating my blood until it boils.

When Luminita's hands rise to the clasp at her neck, my arm stiffens around the girl and my teeth sink deeper. The shimmering fabric falls to Luminita's waist, and the small ruby glints between her bare breasts like a beacon…calling to me.

"Hearken to my voice, O blessed one." She unfastens the low-slung belt, and the dress pools at her feet, leaving her irresistible body bare to me.

Jenny Allen

The human stops screaming, but I don't care.

"Breathe on me in a spirit of perfect divinity."

My heart beats like a frantic drum. We are standing on a precipice, seconds away from falling, and I *want* to fall. I extract my teeth and shove the unconscious thing to the ground. There is *nothing* between me and my goddess now.

I storm toward her, quickly eating the distance between us while my chest heaves. Her eyes widen and the thrumming energy pulls taut.

The maddening desire that's built over the past two days consumes me. My hands surge past her hair to grip her face and my bloody mouth crashes against hers in a brutal kiss. The collision of souls is absolute and devastating.

Luminita doesn't pull away. She doesn't hide. Her hands bracket my face, pulling me closer while she eagerly returns my kiss. The moan that escapes her is more divine than any other sound I can recall.

My tongue slips past her lips in fervent demand, claiming every inch. She tastes like wine, blood, and magic, and I know with certainty, she is an addiction I will never shake.

Luminita's hands curl around my neck, but it isn't enough. I need her closer. I need to touch every inch…claim every inch…lose my myself buried in her heat.

My hands firmly slide down her hips, her ass, and grip the back of her thighs, hauling her up against me. A wanton moan vibrates through our kiss, and it makes my cock throb with jealously. Luminita wraps her arms around my neck, pressing her chest to mine, and clamps her legs around my waist. It still isn't enough, not when her tongue dances against mine in a rhythm as eager and desperate as my own. I *need* her now.

I lower to my knees and take her to the ground. The sudden rush of excitement from nestling between her thighs forces me to pull my mouth away from hers to catch my breath.

The firelight glimmers on her heated skin, flush with undeniable desire. Those raven curls spill across the ground like a dark halo, and blood smears her delicious mouth. My gaze catches on the ruby pendant…a drop of blood in crystal form, rising and falling with her heavy breaths.

Draga & the Savage: Dragobete

"Draga meu." The whispered words pass my lips in devotion before I claim her mouth again. Driving need compels me to grind against her, my hard length trapped between us, and I break the kiss once more to capture her pebbled nipple. An erotic moan rips from her throat when my teeth graze roughly across the sensitive bud. I want to pull *every* reaction from her…experience *every* sound of pleasure she's capable of until I memorize them all.

My hand slips lower, drawn toward the apex of her thighs, to the heat I crave so deliriously, and she tenses.

"Wait." The breathy plea escapes between panted breaths.

I release her nipple and rock against her while moving my mouth to her ear. "I've waited long enough to find you," I confess. Seven thousand years never knowing what life truly meant…believing nothing held importance but blood…I'm done waiting.

Luminita pushes at my chest until I rise enough to meet her determined eyes. "The wine. You must drink or the rite won't be complete." Desperation tears at her voice. "Please." Tears glisten in those oceans of blue. I may not have her ability to sense emotion, but I feel her fear as if it's my own. I can't refuse her…can't deny her anything.

Reluctantly, I roll onto my side, allowing her to get up. I immediately miss her warmth to an agonizing degree, but at least the view is enticing as she bends to retrieve the chalice and dagger.

When she turns and finds my lustful eyes on her, her gaze quickly falls to the chalice in her hand. She pauses, but only for a moment. The red stone sparkles between her perfect breasts with every step closer. The urge to take her has only heightened since our ravaging kiss. Her magic is in my veins now, compelling me.

As she steps over my legs, I sit up and grab her hips. She pauses again, her wide eyes finally meeting mine, but I can't decipher her expression.

With a gentleness I've never known, I pull her down onto my lap and drag my lips along her neck. Draga trembles beneath the teasing touch before she leans away from me. Her eyes are on the chalice again with the same contemplative expression.

Jenny Allen

Luminita drops the dagger and searches my eyes while she caresses my cheek. When she leans close, her lips hovering above mine, she whispers, "*Sălbatic meu.*"

The fervent kiss brings the insatiable heat right back and her hips roll, grinding against my throbbing cock. I *need* to sink inside her…need it more than blood…more than life.

Luminita breaks the kiss with tears shining in her eyes, seemingly overcome by the moment's significance. She presses the chalice to my lips and begins to chant once more. "In intoxication, physical and spiritual, we recover the intensity of feeling which prudence had destroyed."

Her voice strains, and I drink, enchanted by my fierce goddess and the tears along her dark lashes.

"We find the world full of delight and beauty, and our imagination is suddenly liberated from the prison of everyday preoccupations. Become one with god!"

After draining the cup, I let it fall to the ground. My hand grips her nape, drawing her mouth back to mine. Fingers sink into my hair, her tongue swirls with mine hypnotically, and her body curls, gliding her slick heat along my length still trapped between us. The sensation makes the world spin, and I lock my arms around her waist. Luminita arches her back, soft curls cascading down her back. Rising moans escape her full lips while her body continues to tease me into a frenzy.

The night spins around me in a delirious haze. I haven't even thrust inside her yet and I can't think. The disorientation reaches dizzying heights, and I close my eyes to fight the sensation. My heart beats impossibly fast, blood thunders in my ears, and my chest tightens.

Luminita cups my face while I struggle to breathe. "Aaron, *Sălbatic meu*, look at me." The fear in her voice is what makes me comply. My eyes flutter open to witness her concerned face. Darkness edges into my vision. Something is wrong. I suddenly feel disconnected, lost in a void. I can't feel her warm weight in my arms. It leaves me cold, and then there is only darkness.

19. The Price

Luminita

I watch the unconscious human fall to the ground and my eyes snap up to Aaron's hauntingly brutal face. Wild passion rages in his turbulent eyes, the breeze makes wisps of his long hair dance, and blood still drips from his chin. He is Ares and Dionysus incarnate...Blood and frenzy, and I have never desired someone more. My entire body vibrates with an instinctual urge to move to him...to touch him. Before I can force my body into motion, he storms toward me, quickly closing the distance.

Aaron doesn't hesitate. My eyes widen with the sudden tidal wave of emotion he carries with him. His hands grip my face and I drown in his devotion before his mouth crashes against mine. The culmination of every tease, every flirt along the dangerous line, explodes with a soul consuming intensity far beyond anything I expected. I'm lost to it. Lost to him.

My hands reach out, grabbing his face and drawing him closer. The tang of copper is as intoxicating as the savage himself. When his tongue presses adamantly against mine, a moan travels up my throat, vibrating through the kiss. It only fuels his madness. He invades my mouth, claiming every bit, and I don't just surrender. I welcome it. I want more.

Salacious energy rips through me in a continuous current and my hands slide past his face to grip his neck, keeping him close. But it's not enough for him…or me. His aching desire follows his hands as they slide down the curves of my body. I want his touch everywhere at once. I'm frantic for it.

He grips my thighs and hauls me up into his arms with a terrifying surge of essential need. It rips another wanton moan from me. I need to be closer. I need *him*. My arms and legs wrap around him until our bodies are pressed tightly against each other. I deepen the frenzied kiss, pouring everything into it…lost in a sea of savagery.

I feel him lower, and my back hits the ground, but the weight of him between my thighs sends a primal thrill through my core, soaking me in unbridled desire.

Aaron ends the brutal kiss, panting for breath. His silvery eyes stare down at me with such wonder…such adoration. *"Draga meu,"* he whispers in heartbreaking devotion, and the first true inkling of fear sneaks in.

Then he claims my mouth once more, drowning my apprehension. The feel of his hard length moving against me as he grinds his hips, ignites every cell in urgent need. I'm still overcome by the sensation when his mouth captures my aching nipple. The delicious and almost painful scrape of his teeth nearly sends me careening over the edge.

When his hand slips lower, seeking my sex, sudden panic steals the breath from my lungs. I am no virgin. I've had sex many times, but always maintained control. I have never been lost to a man as I am right now, and it is wholly terrifying.

"Wait," I gasp in desperation.

His mouth leaves my breast to find my ear and his hips move against me again in a motion that makes my head spin. "I've waited long enough to find you." I feel every bit of the longing and fierceness in his words, but those sensations only scare me more.

I push at his chest with a sudden need to breathe, panic clawing at my insides. "The wine. You must drink or the rite won't be complete," I lie with bone-deep fear rending me. I can't surrender. I can't release control, even if he doesn't mean to harm me. I cannot lose what I have worked three hundred years to gain…my sense of self, my independence, my power, control over my destiny. "Please," I nearly sob.

Draga & the Savage: Dragobete

He relents, rolling off me, and air rushes into my lungs. All my instincts scream for me to run for the chalice, but I move slowly to not arouse suspicion. The aching loss Aaron feels as I walk away rips at me though. To have a creature so old and powerful desire me to such an extent…beyond the physical…is a rare and fragile thing.

One hand wraps around the cool metal of the chalice, the dagger heavy in my other, and I turn back to him. The erotic worship seething in his grey eyes fills me with shame. My gaze falls to the chalice in my hand, and I pause. Am I truly willing to forever destroy this fragile moment? To alter our course? To set us on a path that may drive him from my life?

Sadness wells in my chest as I continue forward. Love is not a luxury I can afford, as much as I may want it…as much as I crave the release of giving myself to him. That future only ends with my submission.

When I step over his legs, his warm hands are suddenly on my hips, and the torrential flood of devout affection rips through me. My wide eyes meet his with all the intensity of the first kiss we shared, and I falter. He guides me down to his lap with a gentleness I never thought him capable of and lips trail over my neck. The softness makes me tremble.

It would be so easy to let go…to surrender.

I lean back, staring down at the chalice in my hand. If I do this, there is no going back. I can never reclaim this night, our first union. Everything that has happened between us will be forever tainted.

The dagger falls from my hand, and I caress his cheek, searching his eyes for some truth that might stop me…some sign that surrender doesn't mean submission. But he is a man, in a man's world. Women are property, possessions…nothing more. There is no recourse. No way to have control and still give in. I know that if I have him now, like this, it will ruin me.

I lean forward with my heart fracturing in my chest. "*Sălbatic meu*," I whisper against his lips. It's most likely the last time I will be able to call him that. Every emotion and deep desire infuses my kiss, and my hips roll, savoring the feel of him. Heady desire roars through me and I break the kiss.

I have no choice. Tears sting my eyes as I press the chalice to his lips. The adoring expression he wears only deepens the cracks in my heart. The chanted words barely pass my constricted throat. "In intoxication, physical and spiritual, we recover the intensity of feeling which prudence destroyed."

The false words feel bitter on my tongue. I am using prudence to destroy intensity…to save myself. Tears spill down my cheeks and I force myself to continue. "We find the world full of delight and beauty, and our imagination is suddenly liberated from the prison of everyday preoccupations. Become one with god!"

My heart withers as I watch him drain the chalice, his ravenous eyes never leaving mine. Fresh panic screams in my head, wishing I could take it back, undo this death blow to both our hearts. His hand grips my neck and I'm drawn back to him, our mouths colliding once more.

For the moment, he is still Aaron, and I devour every precious second. I deepen the kiss, curl my body to slide along his impressive length, drink in every ounce of carnal awe and genuine adoration while they still exist. The overwhelming emotions arch my back, ripping moans from me while I rock against him.

His arm clamps around my waist, clinging to me and I feel the first twinges of disorientation. Fresh tears flood my eyes as panic quickly builds within him. His eyes are closed.

I'm overtaken by the desperate need to see him one last time…to see the intense passion, the wide-eyed devotion, the only man who has mattered to me. "Aaron, *Sălbatic meu*, look at me."

His silvery eyes open and I watch in renewed horror as the light leaks from them. They become vacant of everything but frenzy and madness, and I weep, pressing my forehead to his.

Sălbatic's lips find mine in urgent demand, but the kiss lacks everything that made it special and the final dredges of my heart shatter.

Our bodies move and react…his feral thrusts drive some part of my hunger, but the music of our souls is gone. The ritual act feels hollow and soured even as our erotic cries fill the air. The release is physically divine, but emotionally devastating.

My freedom comes at a price…and it has irrevocably broken us both.

20. Shredded Soul

Aaron

Pain tears through my skull as my eyes squint against the morning sun. My fingers gently prod my scalp in search of a wound but find none. I open my eyes again, but the light sends shards of agonizing pain tearing through my mind, and I squeeze them shut again. I don't remember *ever* feeling like this.

I try to recall what might have happened, but only flashes return to my mind through the rending torment. One clear moment snaps into place. My blood-stained mouth colliding with Luminita's in a kiss that is seared into my very soul, the one I never I knew I had. Perhaps I didn't have one until last night.

In a sudden rush, as if the rest of my body is only now awakening, I feel the ache of every muscle and a sharp pain in my chest. This time I force my eyes open with growing concern. If something happened, if we were attacked...

I peer down to see Luminita's head resting on my shoulder, and I simply watch her breathe for a few moments. The sight brings a mixture of relief and desire. Her naked body is curled against my side, wearing only the gold arm bands, matching necklace, and the small tear-shaped ruby. Wild black curls frame her face in frenzied beauty, and I reach out to touch them. Stinging pain stops me.

Blood smears my chest to the right of my heart and I frown at the sight in confusion. Luminita mentioned something about a sigil… requiring my blood, but I can't remember her carving it. I can't remember much, actually.

Once again, I search through my memories. I recall laying her on the ground, my hips rocking against hers, the maddening moans she released, tears in her eyes. I pause on that thought. Tears. Why?

A sudden bought of nausea wracks me and bile burns up my throat. I turn away from her quickly, getting to my hands and knees as I wretch. The pain in my head only worsens and the meager contents of my stomach spill across the ground. Another new experience for me, one I could have done without.

Wine and Salvia have never affected me this way. Nothing has. Ever.

"Aaron?" Her concerned voice coupled with the rare use of my chosen name draws my attention and I peer over my shoulder at her. She hovers nearby but doesn't touch me. She looks…frightened. "Are you alright?" she asks in a hesitant voice.

"No," I mutter as another wave of pain slices through my skull. "What…happened?"

Silence is my only answer.

Once the agony subsides to a tolerable level, I sit on the ground and stare at her, but she still says nothing. The woman sits there, rigid, but her breaths quicken.

I rub at my temples and dig through my memories again—torchlight flickers over her creamy skin as she holds the chalice to my lips, tears fall down her cheeks, dizziness, then darkness.

My gaze shifts up to her with a growing sense of apprehension. "What did you put in the wine?"

The delicate column of her throat shifts and it tears a gaping chasm in my chest.

"What did you do?" I barely manage to ask the question. All the awe and passion of last night rush back through me. Our savage kiss…our collision of souls…haunts me as I stare into the bottomless depths of her blue eyes, searching for truth.

Draga & the Savage: Dragobete

Luminita sits back, drawing her legs to her chest, hiding. Her gaze slips from mine. "Ritual herbs."

Even I can sense the lie and it summons a fury that rivals the splitting ache in my head. "Do not lie to me, Draga," I state firmly in an attempt to control my anger.

The title seems to wound her, and she shrinks in on herself. "It is not a lie." Her voice is soft...distant, and I surge to my feet.

Luminita's blue eyes widen, snapping up to me, and the fear returns to them.

"What else?" I snarl.

The woman watches me, her chest quickly rising and falling as if on the edge of panic.

"What else?" I repeat, taking a step closer.

Luminita rises to her feet, her eyes locked on me, but then she turns away. Turns away from *me*. Pain, anger, and nausea rise in equal measure, and I double over, dragging in deep breaths. When the sickness subsides, I glare up to see her fastening her dress, and my feeble control snaps.

I storm over, snatching her arm, and yank her around to face me. "What did you put in the wine, Luminita?"

She stares up at me with tears shining in her eyes. "Datura seeds."

My heart plummets and I feel as if it's nicked by every rib on the way down. With growing horror, I push her away from me. "You tried to poison me?"

"No!" she cries, grabbing my arm. "No. I didn't want to hurt you."

Rage burns in the hollow pit of my chest. "What *did* you want?" I snap through gritted teeth.

Her head shakes, she swallows hard, but her teary gaze falls to the ground. "The rite...it requires frenzy."

More lies. I grab both her arms in a tight grip and lean down to crowd her vision. "Was my passion not frenzied enough?"

My snarling question makes her flinch. The truth of what happened hits me then. Datura seeds are not only used for poison. In the correct dosage, they are also used to break a man's will...to separate his consciousness so that only the beast remains. My stomach sickens all over again.

"You drugged me…" I shove her away and she stumbles. "You drugged me so you could have your savage *without me*."

Once again, Luminita's tear-filled gaze falls to the ground, and it's the only confirmation I need. My head hangs low as a torrent of emotion rages war inside me. Everything from rejection to despair to wrath burns in me and for the first time in my recollection, tears sting my eyes. It only fuels my rage.

My hand is wrapped around her delicate throat before another thought can form. "Did you enjoy your beast? Was it better that way?" I snarl the words in utter contempt as her eyes widen.

Luminita adamantly shakes her head, her throat shifts with a hard swallow, but she says nothing.

"You *stole* that moment from me, corrupted it like a fucking devil."

Light glints off the blooddrop stone over her heart and my rage is all consuming. I snatch the pendant and yank, breaking the chain, and her entire body stiffens. Fresh tears stream down her face and despite everything, it cuts at me.

I lean closer until my breath mingles with hers and close my eyes against blinding tears. "Why would you do this?" My throat constricts around the words nearly breaking my voice. "I would have given you everything." My forehead leans against hers while pain, anger and heartache shred my insides. "I would have knelt at your feet…willingly. Worshipped you."

A strangled sob escapes her lips, and her hand caresses my cheek. For one selfish moment, I lean into the touch and mourn my loss.

Then I shove her to the ground, and turn away, unable to even look at her. Anger carries me toward the river. I stalk through the clearing, past the trees. The growing sound of the Mureș' rushing waters echoes the deafening roar in my head, drowning out everything else.

A hand grips me and I rip my arm away, intent on my destination. She says something, but I can't hear it. The demoness steps in my path and the glare I level at her is filled with icy wrath.

"Stop, Sălbatic."

Draga & the Savage: Dragobete

The word fills me with hate. "Do *not* call me that. You had your savage. *I* wasn't enough."

Her face crumples and her palms touch my chest. "No. That's not true."

I shove her hands away. "I don't care." With a menacing glower I march past her.

"That's not true either," she calls after me, and I hear her hurried footsteps following me.

"Then I'll hate you until it's true."

The footsteps behind me falter for a moment, and then she runs to grab my hand. "No! Aaron."

Rage turns my vision red, and I whirl on her. "What do you want that you haven't already taken?"

Her chest heaves beneath the crimson fabric and I loathe the way it makes me still want her. "None of that is why," she cries.

My gaze snaps to her tear-streaked face and I take a step closer, making her back up. "Then why?"

Luminita's mouth opens but she says nothing.

I take another step, rage heating my blood. "Explain it to me!"

She shakes her head with tears still filling her eyes. "You can't understand."

My blood boils in my veins until red is all I see. *"Then chose to make me understand or I will force you to."* I snarl every word with venom.

Luminita's demeanor shifts suddenly, her spine stiffening, and her tears turn to fury. "You will *force me* to do nothing!"

In one quick motion, without conscious thought, my hand grips her throat tight. A small gasp escapes her lips at first, but then her eyes lift to mine in fiery vengeance. Her nails dig into my wrist, and my grip tightens until she draws in mere wisps of air. Then I feel it. The pull.

Sudden weakness cripples me and I'm on my damn knees before her. She rips my hand away from her throat and her sharp glare cuts through me. It reminds me of her self-proclaimed title—Eater of Souls—and that's precisely what she is. Luminita...my Goddess of blood and chaos...brought my soul to life and consumed it in one night.

Jenny Allen

"Why stop? Drain the life from me like those peasants. I'm obviously no better to you."

The growling words make her flinch, and she takes several steps back from me. I watch her, disgusted by my own confliction. Even now...I still want her.

After swallowing hard, I get to my feet and turn away from her again. The river is close. I storm toward it with the pendant squeezed so tightly in my fist I feel it break the skin. I don't know if she follows me. I can't hear anything but the roar of water and the pounding of my fractured heart.

When I reach the river's edge, I stare down at the ruby in my bloody palm. The shredded remnants of my fledging soul mourn everything it represents. My vision blurs with angry tears and I rear back, throwing the cursed thing into the river.

21. The Weight

Luminita

Aaron turns his back on me, and marches toward the river. I'm still frozen in place when I watch him throw the necklace into the rushing waters with a primal scream that rips through me. Any remnants in my aching chest turn to ash, and my fingers drift to my throat where his blind rage still lingers on my skin. I wonder how long the impression will last. For the first time in my life, I wish I didn't have the ability to sense emotional imprints. How long will the sensation of his overwhelming heartbreak, fury, and hatred haunt me? A day? A year? A lifetime? Longer?

I did this. I created this carnage…summoned his wrath…betrayed the trust he thinks he had in me, but I was right to do so. *Then chose to make me understand or I will force you to.* Aaron's violent words repeat in my head while I walk back to the ritual site…the place where my heart took its last breaths and died.

When pushed, Aaron tried to dominate me, to *force* what he wanted from me. For all his supposed devotion and claims of worship, he is still a man. Worse. He's had thousands of years to ingrain his inherent dominion over the *fairer* sex.

A tiny voice, weak and brittle in the back of my mind, tries to tell me it's not true, but I can't listen to it. I can't face the alternative.

Jenny Allen

I change into my simple shift and black vest before angrily balling up the dress and gold pieces into my makeshift pack. They may be a birthright, but right now I don't want to see them. The sight sickens me. They only remind me of my foolishness…my reckless dalliance with an impossible belief. No man will ever see me as an equal. I know that with certainty now.

As I make my way through the clearing, I pause by the silver chalice gleaming in the morning sun. The last of my tears fall. I may have put the poison in the wine and placed it at his lips, but it only hastened our inevitable destruction. I was something new, a mystery to solve, a rarity he would tire of, and eventually he'd resort to the same sense of entitlement and ownership all men lord over women. *Or I will force you to.* His words are seared into my mind as a constant reminder of that.

I leave the chalice behind. I can't bring myself to touch it. If by some horrific trick of fate, I am wrong…the wicked thing would only serve as a reminder of the reality I chose. I pass the krater, which still smolders, and the young maidan whose lifeless eyes greet the sky.

At the clearing's edge, I gaze back at the wreckage left behind. Aaron hasn't emerged from the woods. Perhaps he never will. Watching him throw the ruby pendant into the river may be the last time I see him. That would probably be best for both our sakes.

Then I will hate you until it's true. The angry words still haunt me because I know they are as real as the lingering rage on my throat. Even if I was wrong…even if I recklessly acted out of fear…what's done is done. There is no undoing it. Whatever he felt for me has twisted into something ugly.

I close my eyes and see him bathed in torchlight, his long hair wild, blood smearing his mouth, an overwhelming well of lustful worship burning bright in his stormy eyes. It seems the chalice didn't claim the last of my tears after all. If only we could have lived in that magical moment…a god and goddess above the notions of control and dominion…true equals, but that is not the way of the world.

Never again will I allow myself to believe in such foolish notions. There is only survival…whatever the cost. *Prostul moare de grija alutia—* The fool dies worrying about someone else.

Draga & the Savage: Dragobete

Despite the ritual, the energy we created, the strength I ripped from Aaron, I feel weary. The power ebbs and flows in my veins, but even that is a weight on my battered soul. I want nothing more than to sleep for weeks. My eyes drift to the ground after the thought. Perhaps there is one thing I want more. One impossible thing. An unobtainable thing. The weight only worsens.

The trudge back to town is a lonely one, at least for a while. When I near the city, children laugh and play among the trees, searching for flowers in honor of Dragobete. A few tug at my skirt and hold up the snowdrops and crocus they've found. I pay them no mind, walking steadily forward as if in a trance.

The tavern is just as crowded as it was last night, but I barely feel the groping hands as I pass. Let them have their cheap thrill. Their lives are so short. My hand drifts to my throat again…to the rage still clinging there, and for one burning moment, I am jealous of their brief existence. They don't carry the weight of ghosts. They aren't haunted for centuries by the fury and agony in someone's touch.

I pace up the stairs, shoving every ounce of emotion into a deep, dark pit where it belongs. Survival requires it. Feel nothing. Give nothing. Do what is necessary. Survive the patriarchy. Rise above the humans' meager existence. Embrace my role as a true Goddess of blood and chaos, merciless and ruthless. Those are my life lessons. That is the only way to carry the overwhelming weight in my chest and endure the savage rage seared into my flesh.

22. Gone

Aaron

The afternoon sun warms my back as I finally set foot in Deva, but the icy water from the river has left a chill in my bones. Then again, perhaps the Mureș is not responsible for that cold ache. For seven thousand years…the rise and fall of so many kingdoms…the span of millions of human lives, I cared about nothing but blood and embracing my violent nature.

Part of me wishes that were still true. If I hadn't followed the Mongol Horde…hadn't stayed in that hut…hadn't met *her*, I wouldn't have to feel this brutal chasm in my chest. It's probably to my detriment, but the part of me that longs for the callous calm is but a tiny piece.

I trudge up the stairs of the inn, revisiting my realization on the riverbank. Even the agony of having a moment I desired with such intensity stolen from me, the betrayal, the vicious anger in her oceanic eyes…none of it can sway me from her. I knew it during the rite. She is an addiction from which I cannot recover.

The pain is better than feeling nothing at all, and Luminita Dragomir is the only creature to truly inspire me…to move me to *tears*…to make me believe in magic…to tear my soul wide open when I didn't know I even had one.

The sad fact is…I'd rather endure her wrath and torment than walk the world without her. I'd settle for some small sliver of her than nothing at all. She sees me, knows me, accepts me even if she won't allow herself to love me for some reason. I couldn't get the truth from her about why she drugged me.

Perhaps I'd become too soft…worshipped her too much. Maybe I simply was not savage enough for her ritual. *Not enough.* It's a concept I have never cared about until now. Of course, I have never cared about anyone's opinion, not even my brothers' until I met my goddess.

When I reach the door to our room, it feels like my throat tightens around my pounding heart. I simply stare at the rough wood, trying to draw in breath. Luminita may simply drain me like those peasants the night we met. This could be the end of my nearly eternal life. If so, it would be a worthy end. Some small part of me would be forever with her and I'd die having experienced something real.

After dragging in a deep breath, I rap my knuckles upon the wood. The sound seems to echo through the room with unsettling finality.

There is no answer and my heart races a little faster. Would she simply dismiss me? Not even grant me the opportunity to lay eyes on her? The image of her tear-streaked face haunts me. She cried. Was it merely an act or did she regret her decision?

I knock again, louder this time. Still, there is no answer, and a horrible sinking feeling knots my stomach. I try the door and find it unlocked. When I swing it open, the room is empty and another shard of my dying soul fractures. The cast iron mortar and pestle sit beneath the table—the one she used to crush the Datura Seeds that sealed our fate—and her laurel crown sits upon the bed, but there is nothing else.

My vicious goddess of blood and chaos is gone, and I have no means to find her.

I pace the small space and sink onto the bed…the one we shared. The image of her gorgeous face pressed against my shoulder in peaceful slumber surges to the forefront of my thoughts and fresh tears burn my eyes. She has doomed me twice over. First, she stole the memory of our first union…tore away the only thing I truly craved, and now she has cursed me to walk the world without her, carrying the weight of that loss.

Draga & the Savage: Dragobete

I wipe the infernal tears from my cheeks and grab the laurel crown from the mattress. My fingers caress over the leaves with the memory of her sitting in the chair, teasing me as she weaved it, and I find myself wondering if any of it was real. I know, deep down, it was, but admitting that fact...embracing it...hurts too much.

I glance down at the small sigil carved into my chest—a cup holding three grapes...the sign of Dionysus. My fingertips trace the healing cuts longingly. There is only one solution to my problem. I have to find her. I need the truth from her, even if it ultimately leads to my destruction. Life without *Draga meu* in some form is not a life I wish to lead any longer.

This epic tale continues in
Draga & the Savage: Dracul- Part 1

Continue to the next page for a sneak peek
at the first two chapters.

Excerpt from
Draga & the Savage:
Dracul – Part 1

1. A Smaller World

Luminita

Suceava – October 1448

Since leaving Deva that fateful night over two hundred years ago, the world has gotten smaller. Villages became towns, towns turned into cities, castles and fortresses of stone now dot the landscape, and it has become harder to hide.

The legends of Dragaica have dwindled to mere stories, and the rising prominence of the Roman Catholic and Orthodox Churches have brought rumors of savage witch trials. Not only are people less inclined to believe in my readings and performances, but those things have also become dangerous. Any display of my power, even in self-defense is a risk, and I am no longer capable of sustaining myself as I have for hundreds of years.

The world is changing, and I must adapt. Avoiding humans is no longer the best way to control my fate. I must hide among them, stealing small bits of emotion unnoticed. I must plot and scheme, navigate the political waters, manipulate things to my advantage, and take an active part in shaping my world.

Unfortunately, this requires a man.

Unmarried women are capable of little more than the *tigani boieresti*—the Roma slaves belonging to the powerful boyar families, the royal lines who own the land. As with unmarried women, they are legally *human*, not property, but hold no rights.

I loathe the concept of even feigning the appearance of submission and adopting the demure etiquette required by the courts. I am an ancient Goddess of blood and chaos among the weak, but survival is all that truly matters. I have sacrificed for it before…

My fingers trace along my neck and the fragile imprint barely detectable upon my skin. The fury and hatred was so palpable once…the curse I was forced to endure because of my actions on Dragobete so many years ago.

However, over time, the imprint of his emotions became a comfort, a reminder of his existence, and a warning to never again consider granting a man true power over me.

My thoughts often drift to my Savage, wondering if he still stalks the earth. In all these years, we have never again crossed paths, and I could not bring myself to look for him.

With a heavy sigh, I smooth the lines of my red dress. The corset and square neckline show enough cleavage to be enticing without being risqué. An oval ruby rests in the hollow of my throat, suspended on a gold chain. The stone is the wrong shape, but that is best. A reminder of what is lost forever will not help me advance my schemes.

I can play a part among these short-lived humans and pull the prideful strings of men. The politics may be more complex, but individual men are easy to manipulate.

Draga & the Savage: Dracul- Part 1

Part of crafting the illusion required choosing a name more befitting of a delicate maidan. Luminita has been a whisper among the people, nearly synonymous with Dragaica, and the noble Dragomir name still intimidates some.

For this particular dance to succeed, I must be underestimated. While that is an inherent result of being a beautiful, seemingly young woman in these times, orchestrating events in the Suceava court in Moldova takes a delicate hand and an innocent façade, which cannot be called into question.

The persona of Katharina Siegel, the daughter of the Weaver's Guild noble south of Bucharest, is the definition of lilting femininity. She dances with lords, whispers sweet things, and takes advice from *older* women of repute. It disgusts me to no end, playing this part each night, but I have no choice in this patriarchal dictatorship.

In the past few months since arriving in Suceava, I've caught the eye of several nobles, three of whom have proposed marriage, but none of them carry enough clout to tempt me. Re-marrying is near impossible. I must choose my target carefully or risk falling victim to my own schemes.

Not a single one has possessed the strength I truly crave. My brief time in Deva left me desperate for the challenge...for a man to pose a true threat...for a worthy opponent. Of course, no human man is capable of that. It is likely an itch I will never again scratch.

I have not encountered another strigoi and I have avoided the other Durand. The males of my kind are even more callous and ruthless toward women than humans. Therefore, I am forced to find contentment in the minds of simple human men.

New arrivals are expected at tonight's feast, according to the new Moldovan Voivode, Peter the third. He began his rule after deposing Roman the second, who was a mere twenty-two years of age. Peter is not much older and has a rather loose tongue when it pertains to court gossip.

According to the Voivode, a Wallachian noble who failed to take back his usurped throne is due to arrive tonight, seeking asylum in his court. The newcomer does not sound promising, but I have been surprised before...once at least.

After caressing my neck, savoring the final traces of the imprint, I straighten and pull on the mask of polite innocence I've carefully crafted. Whatever it takes to secure my future…to control my fate…to survive. No price is too high.

My fingertips drift between my breasts where a tear-shaped ruby once dangled. The ghost of it still clings to my skin. I've proven the price I'm willing to pay for my freedom…my heart and soul. Love is fleeting, but I have the potential for eternal life, even if it's as nothing more than a wicked creature pulling strings to achieve power. After all, power enables survival where love only puts it at risk.

2. Bogdan

Aaron
Kosovo Polje – October 1448

I strongly dislike retreat. Allowing *humans* to chase me away is a personal insult after seven thousand years as a vampire. I'm not the only one, but I am the oldest. Yet here I am, retreating from a sea of soldiers.

I grip the sword tighter as we race through the forest. The blood coating every inch of my body feels tacky, and my muscles burn. After three grueling days of fierce battle and losing far too many men, the Voivode of Wallachia and Regent of Hungary, John Hunyadi, called for the retreat.

I have never respected a human. Their lives are too brief to even garner my interest most times, but John is the closest a human has come to earning my regard. War is in his blood, and his strategic mind is sharper than most. Well, perhaps not in this specific instance.

This time, he underestimated the Ottoman forces and their allies. They overwhelmed us. No overwhelm is too generous a word. It was slaughter. Thousand upon thousands of our men died.

Now John and I are racing for Beszterce with only a handful of men.

Chaos and the clang of swords erupt to my right flank…John's direction. I swerve toward the conflict, sprinting like a blood-soaked devil between the evergreens. As I fly toward the fray, my left hand touches my armor and the small object hidden beneath the scales at the center of my chest. It's habit anymore, especially when facing danger. I've already suffered life's deepest wounds and my heart still beats.

When I burst into the small clearing, John and three of his men are surrounded but still fighting. These are not soldiers of the Ottoman Empire, however. The color accenting their chainmail and tunics identify them as Serbian. Fantastic. Another one of John's enemies.

Without hesitation, I grip the pommel of my sword with both hands and slash up, catching the first soldier under the helmet. The brutal hit against the chainmail vibrates up my already weary arms, but the man's head flops to his shoulder with a sickening crack before he crashes to the ground.

Two men rush in my direction, side by side, and I don't hide my wicked smile as I relax into a fighting stance. When they're close enough, I parry the first blow, spinning to thrust my sword straight into the second man's throat, the blade scraping the jawbone before hitting his spine.

I don't hear the gargled sounds as he chokes, but the warmth from the blood splashing my skin when I yank the sword free makes my grin widen. The first soldier recovers his balance and lunges at me. I easily dodge the blow and hack downward with my blade with such power, the metal helmet dents deep, cracking his skull. Blood pours down his face and his body thuds to the ground.

A sharp sting at my thigh has me spinning to block another slicing cut. Our swords clang, and the man tries to push back. A waste of time. I slam my armored fist into his face, breaking the stalemate, and shove my blade up under his chin until the tip hits the inside of his helmet.

"Bogdan!" John shouts.

I use my boot to shove the Serb off my sword and move deeper into the melee, following John's voice. I sustain a few nicks while trudging through but take out five more men. They aren't as well trained as my recent opponents. The Serbs counted on numbers to overtake us.

I break through the line and see John being carted off. Apparently, numbers won after all.

Draga & the Savage: Dracul- Part 1

At least a dozen men still swarm the area...all targeting me. An absolutely ruthless grin splits my blood-soaked face. The odds are *not* in their favor. I am Aaron, Bogdan the gift of god, Sălbatic the Savage, The Great Barbarian of Wallachia. Blood is what I crave, and I will drink my fill today.

About the Author

Jenny Allen (Deardorff), the author of The Lilith Adams Series, also published poems and short stories in University journals while spending time as a reporter and photographer for the Chattanooga State College newspaper. Ms. Allen studied forensic science, compiled extensive research in world myths, and applied them into a thrilling supernatural series. Her background as a published photographer and award-winning artist helps her visualize scenes when writing, contributing to her unique style of vivid imagery.

Born on a Royal Airbase in Lakenheath, England, she left the U.K. at age nine to travel the United States and Germany. In her sophomore year, she began writing poetry after the suicide of a close friend. She later graduated to short stories and narratives until, in 2002, she wrote her first novel, Lilith in London, which was never published but still exists as 432 handwritten pages. Over twelve years, it underwent a metamorphosis, eventually becoming her first published novel, Blood Lily.

Currently, Mrs. Allen (Deardorff) lives in York, Pennsylvania with her husband, Eric Deardorff, and their two sons, Kaidan and River. When not working as a full-time RN, she is writing and plotting the remaining novels in the main series, the novella series, and the spin-off series with Tim and Eileen, all in the same world.

9 798989 249244